A MADE IN JERSEY NOVEL

THROWN
Down

A MADE IN JERSEY NOVEL

THROWN
Down

TESSA BAILEY

Entangled Publishing, LLC
2614 South Timberline Road
Suite 105, PMB 159
Fort Collins, CO 80525
rights@entangledpublishing.com

Brazen is an imprint of Entangled Publishing, LLC.

Edited by Heather Howland
Cover design by Heather Howland
Cover photo from Sara Eirew

Manufactured in the United States of America

First Edition April 2016

**ENTANGLED
BRAZEN**

Dear Reader,

Here is the beautiful thing about *Thrown Down* to me: life still won't be perfect at the end for River and Vaughn. It will be happy as hell. But not perfect. Dreams don't come true overnight and that's why the *Made in Jersey* series is so special to me. The couples are a work in progress.

Love is a wonderful, messed up business, right? When you throw your lot in with another human being, you will be ironing out wrinkles, over and over again, for the rest of your lives. Money is an issue. For everyone. And sometimes, your only option is to work at a factory or put on an uncomfortable tie and answer to a boss. But you get up every day and iron out those wrinkles, because who the hell wants a perfectly, starched shirt all the time? They itch.

Tessa

For the Babes

Prologue

"How much longer?"

Vaughn De Matteo groaned the words into River Purcell's sweaty neck. This was it. His life was over. Or beginning. Fuck if he knew. His world had been whittled down to one incredible fact—the girl he'd been in love with since time began—or so it seemed—was beneath him in a rucked up prom dress.

And she was minutes from turning eighteen.

"I…" The breathy music of her voice warmed his ear. "The clock s-says two more minu—" She broke off on a cry when Vaughn got pumping again, thrusting his abused cock up against the lace barrier of her panties, creaking the motel room bed springs. Christ. They'd been at this for an hour. Vaughn getting worked up and River soothing him back down. To wait.

"Who did you dance with dressed like this?" His voice had gone hoarse, scraped, tortured. "You look like some kind of fairy."

"Only because I knew I'd see you afterward," River whispered, pushing back the hair that fell into his face. "I don't dress up for anyone else."

Vaughn's laugh sounded agonized as he dragged his forehead down the center of River's body—through her cleavage, down past the labored flutter of her belly button, stopping at the source of his baser lust, his frustration. River's pussy. He hated himself for calling it such a vulgar name when those crucial minutes hadn't ticked past yet, but Vaughn reasoned he'd earned that liberty by refusing to fuck his younger girlfriend for two painful years.

"One more minute, Vaughn."

He exhaled a curse between her legs. "You dress up for me, huh? The no-good prick who can't afford nothin' but a cheap place that rents by the hour?" After finally securing one of the condoms he'd brought around his hurting flesh, Vaughn curled his hands around River's lifted knees, unable to stop his lips from gliding over the swath of pink lace. "Ah, God. You sure you want this, doll?"

River's fingers tugged at his hair, urging him back up her body. "You're the stubborn one who made us wait. I've wanted nothing but *this since my sophomore year. Nothing but you."*

With those blue eyes shining up at him, those unbelievable words hanging in the air, Vaughn couldn't have refrained from kissing River if world peace depended on it. How'd I get this lucky? I shouldn't have gotten this lucky. *Senior class presidents from educated families didn't date thieving dropouts with no future. No one had clued her in?*

When Vaughn finally managed to tear himself away from the frantic kiss, she surprised him by dropping the pink panties onto the bed beside them. "Time's up."

He cupped his girl's cheeks, careful not to abrade her skin with the roughness of his palms. "I love you so damn bad, River Purcell."

"I love you, too." Her voice was unsteady, her fingers tunneling in his hair. "I'll never, ever stop."

Vaughn double-checked the digital bedside clock—

midnight—before fusing their mouths together. As both of them whispered oh God, oh God, oh God, *Vaughn bared his teeth against River's swollen lips and pushed through her virginity. His prolonged growl of pleasure was eventually followed by River's, and the bed springs and distant sounds of televisions blaring joined them to create a symphony all their own.*

Chapter One

Vaughn De Matteo rested his forehead on the steering wheel of his truck and counted to ten. And then he did it again. The process hadn't been necessary since his early twenties—before the army had wrung the hair-trigger temper out of him—but he slipped back into the calming countdown without missing a beat, attempting to ease the anger jabbing into his gut like splinters.

Not anger at the girl—now a woman—he'd left behind in Hook, New Jersey. Jesus, anger and River Purcell didn't even belong in the same vicinity. No, this rage was directed at something bigger than the both of them.

Fate? Nah. Such a lofty title gave the cosmic fuckery too much credit. Karma, maybe. Although, if finding out the woman he'd left behind—for her own damn good—had borne his child, *reared* his three-year-old child *alone*...if this was his comeuppance for touching River in the first place, he deserved it.

"Go ahead, karma," Vaughn muttered. "Do your worst."

His laugh was humorless. As if the situation could *get*

any worse. It had taken him twenty-four hours to absorb the shock wrought by the letter sent by River's brother, Sarge. Twenty-four hours he couldn't really afford, considering the damn piece of correspondence had been sitting in his PO box for months, collecting dust. Although, what was one more day compared to four years, right?

Still numb head to toe, he'd managed to phone his employer for whom he worked as private, armed security detail, relinquishing the steady job he'd fought to procure. The job that allowed him to maintain his empty, colorless lifestyle in Baltimore, nursing whiskey and haunted by memories in a functional one-bedroom apartment overlooking a rail yard. The kind of place he belonged.

After quitting, he'd been on the road within the hour, driving back to Hook, crossing the town limit he'd never thought to darken with his shadow again. Now he sat in the parking lot outside the Kicked Bucket, mere moments from laying eyes on River again, and...fuck. *Fuck.* After not allowing himself to feel anything for so long, after self-medicating with liquor every time the pain got too intense, there was no easing into the idea of being close to her again. Just knowing the filthy stucco structure in his rearview mirror had the nerve to contain River, he could feel the dangerous heating of his blood.

She shouldn't be in there. She shouldn't be in this shitty goddamn town at all. Unknowingly, he'd left her without a choice, though, and now nothing would stand in the way of him repairing the damage, starting with entering the lounge and calmly asking River to speak with him in private. He could handle that, couldn't he? Could manage the task of entering the premises and conducting a reasonable conversation, even though a primal roar had been building in his throat since he'd opened the letter from Sarge.

His River. A mother...an *abandoned* single mother.

And therein lay the reason Vaughn couldn't make himself leave the truck. Because she had to hate him. Hell, she had every right. But living with the memory of her crying on their motel bed—the same bed where he'd taken her virginity—had been painful enough to live with. Adding hatred to heartbreak might just kill him.

No choice, De Matteo. Move.

If Vaughn's reluctance to respond even to his own command wasn't a testament to his passionate dislike for authority, he didn't know what was—one of the main reasons he hadn't been a good fit for the army, no matter how often his superiors had attempted to tell him differently.

"Enough stalling," Vaughn said to his own reflection in the driver's side window, before pushing open the door and exiting. His boots weighed seven tons apiece as he traversed the trash-strewn parking lot, gazing out at the surrounding high-rise apartment buildings. The Kicked Bucket was in a shitty part of town, the nearby residences lacking care. But hey, at least those people could afford a place to raise a family, right? At least they were trying. More than he could have done for River, that was for damn sure.

A few yards from the entrance, he was brought up short when one of the vehicles caught his eye. River's red Pontiac. She still had it? Why did that make him feel as though his intestines were being sucked out through a straw?

Probably because he'd made love to River so many times in the backseat, her tight body riding him, those bee-stung lips wide open as she moaned, they'd happily lost count. Ungrateful for the punishment of his memory, Vaughn slapped the lounge door open with more force than intended. He gave a humorless laugh when none of the regulars so much as flinched. Even though he'd walked in out of the dark, Vaughn's eyes had to make a different kind of adjustment. Smoking might have been outlawed in New Jersey, but the owner had apparently thrown out his ability to give a fuck along with the state regulated No SMOKING signs.

Vaughn peered through the white haze to the stage beyond, where a man performed with an exhausted voice, singing about small town love affairs and tragedy. Tables were scattered in no apparent pattern throughout the joint, filled by amorous couples, or by groups of men, most of them ignoring the musical act in favor of playing cards. Or just plain getting drunk, if the number of empty shot glasses rolling around were any indication.

Shot glasses slowly being collected...by River.

Forty-nine months and three days.

That was how long it had been since he'd seen her.

Vaughn swayed to the right, his shoulder slamming up against the wall. Then he kind of just hung there, counting forward and backward from one to ten. *Not helping. Not helping.* His stomach pitched at the sight of River walking through the drunks, like a nurse walking among the wounded on a battlefield. She could still knock his lights out on sight. Not that he'd doubted it for a second. But God, if it were possible, she'd grown even more beautiful over the last forty-nine months. Her blonde hair was tied up in a ponytail, a pencil stuck through the base, in a way he remembered well enough to make his throat go raw. In a short black skirt and fitted white T-shirt, River tried to look the part of indifferent barmaid, but didn't pull it off. Not by a stretch.

Eyes Vaughn knew were just a shade darker than cornflower blue flitted to each table, and her fingers tugged on the skirt's hem self-consciously every time she approached a new one. When she fumbled with the notepad, recovering with a nervous laugh, a choked sound left Vaughn. "Riv," he whispered.

She looked up so fast, he might as well have shouted. The sudden impact of having River's focus on him after such an extended period of time without it released a rushing sound between his ears, blocking out the sad lounge act… and apparently someone asking if he needed a table. Because when Vaughn snapped back to reality, a man he towered over by at least a foot was in his face. Snapping his fingers.

"I wouldn't…" Vaughn shook his head to clear it, experiencing a resurgence of anger, this time for having his attention diverted from where he needed it to be. On River. "I wouldn't advise snapping your fingers in my face again."

"Why's that, huh?"

A toss of blonde hair snagged Vaughn's gaze as his angelic ex-girlfriend zigzagged through the crowd, drawing more than just *his* notice. Ah no, quite the opposite. She was putting on an unwitting show for every man in the room, attracting lecherous looks by virtue of being her beautiful self, light in a dark tunnel, same way she'd always been.

Fingers snapped in front of his face. *Again.* "This is *my* place and I asked you a question."

"This is *your* place?" Vaughn asked. God, one hour back in Jersey and already his accent had thickened from water to oil. "You hired River Purcell?"

"That's right."

Vaughn plowed a fist into the underside of the man's jaw, watching him fall backward onto the sticky concrete floor with detachment that slowly morphed into satisfaction. *So much for calm*, he thought, shaking out his right hand. Within his chest, he could feel the familiar dark satisfaction that came from fighting. He'd always had it inside him, never gone a day without it. That born and bred edge—passed on by generations of De Matteo men—that should have repelled a young River back in high school.

But no. No, she'd been *drawn,* instead. As she was now, swerving around tables, coming closer to where he stood, still just inside the entrance. She wasn't the only one, either. Men were standing up, cracking their knuckles in the New Jersey state signal for *shit-is-about-to-go-down*. In the corner of his eye Vaughn saw the owner rousing on the floor, noticed him gesturing to the apparently lazy security staff, who also headed in Vaughn's direction. So he did what every levelheaded man would do in a situation where he was outnumbered about two hundred to one.

He lifted his fists, pounding one of them against his chest. "Come on, then," he called out. "Don't be shy as well as stupid."

"Vaughn."

River's voice was breathless as she reached his side, making everything inside him expand like an inflating raft. His fists shook in the air, so he tightened them. *Don't look at her yet, just get her out.* "You got a purse you need to grab or somethin'?"

An expulsion of air came from her lips. "You can't just—"

She broke off when he sent her a look. *The* look. It said, *come on, you remember how I roll. Can't isn't part of my vocabulary.* Placing his attention on River was a mistake, however, because now it couldn't be dragged away by a dozen ox. *Oh Lord.* Those big, sweetheart eyes were tired. Of course, they were. If everything in the letter from Sarge was accurate, she'd been working day shifts at the local factory, in addition to slinging drinks at night.

My fault.

Yeah, his actions were going to cost her this job. Maybe he'd walked into the joint fully aware of that fact. But regret refused to appear. If fifty years had passed since they'd shared oxygen, he would have done the same thing. River belonged in the Kicked Bucket like a virgin belonged in a brothel. As in, she didn't. And he was a presumptuous fucker for assuming the responsibility of that decision, but he'd never claimed to be otherwise. "Hiya, doll."

This was where she coldcocked him. Screamed at him, scratched his eyes out, and told him she hated his guts. *I'm not ready, I'm not ready.*

Turns out he *really* wasn't ready for what happened next.

River's lips lifted in the bright, class president smile he remembered like the back of his hand. So angelic, the other angels in heaven had probably banded together to kick her out. Right onto his unworthy lap. "Hey there, Vaughn." She reached out and patted his shoulder. "Guess you haven't changed much, huh?"

Chapter Two

River had never considered a career in acting, but realized now she might have been shortsighted. Even after months of preparation for Vaughn's return—yes, she'd gone back to blonde and refused to apologize—she hadn't really expected to pull off a warm greeting. After all, this was the man who'd left her broken, bleeding, and sobbing on her knees while he sped off into the night. A woman could take a lifetime to recover from something like that, but in River's case, she thought it might take three. Because while she stood there, smiling up at the son of a bitch, a metal crowbar was doing its damnedest to pry her ribs apart.

Why did he *have* to be so ruggedly gorgeous? His dark blond hair was finger combed, longer than the last time she'd seen it, when he'd rocked an army crew cut. Scruff darkened his cheeks, only adding gravity to his soulful, deep brown eyes. Vaughn had always been in good shape. She remembered watching him do pull-ups on the doorframe of her bedroom, pushups on the floor beside the bed, on nights when he snuck in through the window, or afternoons her parents weren't home. *Burning energy*, he'd called it. Later, she would realize he was working through a reservoir of sexual frustration, but he'd never once pressured her, never made her feel guilty for his painful condition.

River shook the bittersweet memory loose. Yes, Vaughn's arms had always been carved in marble, but they'd expanded beneath the woven together tattoos, barely fitting into the sleeves of his gray T-shirt. His body had settled into manhood with a vengeance, maturing in ways that were not convenient when River needed to remain focused on the plan.

Right, the plan. Get Vaughn to turn around and leave Hook, secure in the knowledge that his presence wasn't needed. Free to go about his business, whatever it was.

He'd fallen off the face of the Earth forty-nine months and three days prior. Unreachable. A lot like he'd been, even when standing right in front of her, all those years ago.

When they'd met in high school, Vaughn's closed off nature had been mysterious. Then she'd graduated Hook High and spent two years taking night classes at the local community college while Vaughn fixed cars to make money— before he'd surprised her by enlisting in the army, staying away for two *more* years, before returning to Hook and leaving her for good, on the very night of his homecoming. That air of mystery had grown stale by then, but she'd been too stubborn to quit attempting to reach him. To beat those walls down with love.

Vaughn rolled his neck, a lot like a boxer entering the ring. If River didn't move soon, one of two things would happen. The crowbar would finish the job it was doing on her ribs, and she'd collapse like a corpse on the floor. Or Vaughn would take on the entire lounge in the most unbalanced fight of the century.

"I know it goes against the De Matteo code," River started, "but I'd appreciate you living to fight another day."

He rolled his big shoulders, appearing to evaluate the approaching men in order to decide on his first victim. "Why is that?"

"I'm the one who cleans up the blood here." She swallowed hard, feeling her mask slip a little. "And I *need* this job, Vaughn."

"You clean up…" He trailed off, taking a long, shuddering breath. "Riv, I can't let you stay here. You know that, right? You know two decades from now, I still won't be over seeing you in this disgusting place."

"Vaughn—"

His gaze was half apologetic, half uncompromising. "Either you quit or I take on all comers. Either way, the mother of my kid isn't working in this place."

Thank God her boss chose that moment to interrupt, because River could hardly breathe under the first acknowledgment of them having a child together. Two invisible pillows pressed against her ears, muffling the bar sounds. Vaughn must have experienced the same shift of gravity, because the intensity radiating from him was palpable.

Destructive.

But it had nothing on the low, brutal hum of guilt that had existed in River's breast since the night Vaughn left.

Focus. She could make up for her impulsiveness if she just stuck to the course of action she'd laid out.

"I thought you didn't have a boyfriend, River," her boss said, in an unfortunate choice of words. At least the man staved off the encroaching wave of customers by holding up a staying hand.

"River having a boyfriend is none of your concern, now is it?" Vaughn massaged one his wrists, the tension packed around him like an aura, growing stronger by the millisecond. "Not that I wouldn't mind hearing an answer myself."

"Don't hold your breath," she sputtered.

Her boss huffed, pacing back and forth behind River. "It is my concern when that boyfriend comes in and assaults me."

"Whatever we are, it's past the boyfriend-girlfriend stage." Vaughn ran a tongue along his bottom lip. "What's it going to be, Riv? We getting out of here?"

What choice did she have? Standing back and allowing innocent—okay, that was pushing it—customers take a beating when she could prevent it would be petulant. With smoke about to whoosh from her ears, River skirted around her boss to retrieve her purse from behind the bar, leaving her apron beneath the register for the morning waitress. Walking back toward Vaughn, she felt time slowing, and molasses churned in her belly. *Don't you dare look at me like that*, she longed to scream in reproof. His dark eyes took in every detail of her appearance in one swoop, that gaze heating considerably the closer she came, as if they were going outside to get sweaty in the Pontiac's backseat, just for old time's sake.

Not on your life, pal.

River could feel every customer's eye on her back as she slipped out the exit, Vaughn close on her heels. "That worked, huh?" Vaughn asked, surprise living within his tone. "You're really just going to leave with me."

"No," River answered, stopping at the driver's side of her Pontiac. "But I thought it would be easier to have a conversation without the angry mob you incited breathing down our necks."

Vaughn appeared thoughtful as he processed that. "So you were expecting me, huh? I guess I should be thankful you knew I would come...once I found out. I never get mail at the PO Box, or I would've been here sooner." He took a step closer, his Adam's apple bobbing, so much heart in his eyes that River's breath suspended in her lungs. "Ah, doll—"

"No." The endearment snapped her spine straight, set her heart galloping around the track of her chest. "I-I mean, yes. I knew you would come. But if I'd had a phone number for you, I would have called to tell you…"

His brawny frame stilled. "Tell me what?"

River forced a smile onto her face. "To tell you how unnecessary it was to travel this whole way." She reached out and gave his rock-hard shoulder a playful shove, ignoring the zap of static. "Vaughn, I have everything under control. Marcy is—"

"Marcy."

Chains rattled in her belly. "You didn't know her name?"

She watched as he went back a few steps, resting against the opposite car. "No. The letter didn't mention it." The eyes from her dreams lifted, snaring her. "I like it, doll. You picked well."

"Please stop calling me that," River whispered, before clearing her throat and willing—with all her might—that positivity surround her like a cloak, hiding everything beneath. "As I said, you are in the clear. We're getting along just fine on our own, and I wouldn't dream of asking you to—"

"Just what the hell is this, River?"

"I'm sorry?"

Vaughn shoved off the opposite car and eliminated the distance between them. River ordered her hands to lift, to stave him off, but they remained useless at her sides, both elbows squeezing against her ribs. Her blood clamored, running with vigor for the first time since Vaughn left. *Damn him. Damn him.* "I'm in the clear?" He repeated her words slowly, as if trying to pronounce the name of a rare disease. "You think I would drive back to Hook at the drop of a goddamn hat because I want to be *in the clear*?"

"I wouldn't presume to know your thought process," River returned with a bemused expression, all the while dying and resurrecting on the inside, in a never-ending pattern. She hadn't tried to find Vaughn upon learning she was pregnant, or even after Marcy was born. She had her reasons for shouldering the responsibility alone—reasons she'd housed inside in an uncrackable safe. They were one and the same with her motives for sending Vaughn packing, as soon as possible.

Raising Marcy alone had been the only option she'd ever allowed herself to consider. She'd built a safeguard against a single iota of dangerous hope for something else filtering in. "Thank you for coming," she whispered. "Thank you for caring, but I've been doing this alone. I…take pride in doing it alone. Please, go. You're free to go."

His breath puffed out on a half laugh, half scoff. "I'm trying to be patient here. God knows I am. But I just found out I have a daughter—a…Marcy. I find out you've been busting your ass to raise her. Alone. *Alone*. And while we're on the subject, you're *not* getting along just fine if you've been working in this shit heap, River. Okay?" He gripped the Pontiac on either side of her head and shook the entire car. "All these years, I thought you were finally in college where you belonged. Instead you've been serving beer to the local drunks."

"You *left*. You left and vanished so you don't *get* an opinion. You don't get to judge what I've done to get by." The words blasted out of her, along with her hands, which pummeled Vaughn in the torso—again and again, harder when he didn't so much as budge or show a reaction. "I hate you. How dare you show up like this, like some hero? Forcing me out of my job and caring. *Caring*. You're the villain, don't you realize that? You left, and you should have stayed gone." Her voice broke. "I hate you so much."

"There we go. There it is. Okay," Vaughn breathed, gathering River's body close, despite her attempts to push him off. Those cannon-size arms banded like steel around her and wouldn't let go, crushing her against his woodsy-smelling chest. "Okay, doll. I know you're right. I…I wasn't a good man to you. I'm still not a good man. But I'm here, and I'm not leaving until we figure out how to handle this between us."

River inhaled a lungful of Vaughn's scent, catching him off guard, which finally allowed her to jerk free of his hold. "I don't need a hero. I'm my own hero now…and I'm trying to be one for Marcy." She groped for the driver's side door handle behind her. "If you ever felt anything for me, Vaughn, you'll turn around and leave Hook."

His gaze cut to the side. "Can't do that, Riv."

Frustration welled within her. "Well, you can't be part of our lives when you never wanted me—" Her cheeks flamed. "*Us.* Never wanted us to begin with."

River got into the car and blew out of the parking lot, trepidation prickling her skin when she glimpsed Vaughn in the rearview mirror—a very determined Vaughn.

And she knew the fight was only beginning.

Chapter Three

River drummed her fingers on the keyboard, waiting for the ancient church computer to catch up with modern technology, also known as the internet. Since she didn't have a computer at home—although she'd been saving for one so Marcy could benefit—Adeline, the choir director, allowed her to use the church's old Dell desktop once a week to Skype with Jasmine.

Her best friend had moved to Los Angeles months ago to be with River's brother Sarge, who had blown back into town with his guitar and turned everyone's day-to-day routine on its head. In an amazing twist, Jasmine was now a vocalist with Old News, Sarge's rock band, and they were preparing for a world tour.

While she couldn't be happier that two of her favorite people were in love and getting ready to marry, River couldn't help but wish—just a little bit—that everything was back the way it had been before last Christmas. Then it had been two best friends against the world, working side by side in the factory every day, Jasmine going on bad dates, River attempting to ignore the lingering specter of Vaughn. She missed having someone read between her lines, knowing her mind without a single word.

Selfish. Stop being selfish. River checked the digital clock in the lower right-hand corner of the screen, willing the computer to work faster so she wouldn't be late for her shift at the factory, where she printed license plates, along with other outsourced products mostly seen on infomercials. It would only be five thirty in the morning in Los Angeles, but Jasmine insisted River call anyway, being that she had no other time options, working two jobs and caring for Marcy.

And now Vaughn was back. River's drumming fingers paused in their vigorous rhythm, and her eyelids slid lower. She'd screwed up last night, erupting up like a volcano of feelings, and she needed to be more careful. Whether she liked it or not, her ex-boyfriend and father of her child had a knack for reading every thought in her head. Telling Vaughn she hated him was counterproductive, immature…and not necessarily true, either. He would see right through her encouragement to leave Hook — to be free of responsibility — and know she wasn't over the past.

Get back on course. That was the revised plan. She'd gone through the sleepless nights, the teething, the potty training with Marcy all on her own. She'd done a good job and would *continue* to do a good job. She would never regret the decisions she'd made that night at the motel — they'd brought her a beautiful little girl that loved her unconditionally — but no way would someone else's life be affected by her actions.

Biting down on the guilt, River sat forward, relieved when Skype began to dial the number she'd entered five minutes ago. Jasmine answered on the first ring, draped in a white bathrobe, a cup of coffee poised at her lips. "Hey, Riv."

"Hey." God, Jasmine looked so happy and content, a rosy glow and tangled hair making it obvious how she'd spent the prior evening. Not that River wanted the details about her brother and best friend's sex life. Although, if the songs they'd been writing together were any indication, things were… pretty darn super in that department. "Sorry for the early call."

"Stop. You apologize every week." Jasmine set down her coffee mug with a click. "How's the kiddo? You haven't texted me a picture in days. Me and Sarge are going through withdrawals."

"Sorry." River fumbled for her cell phone. "I have one with a bowl on her head…milk *still* inside. I can send—"

"What's wrong?"

River looked up to see Jasmine scrutinizing her from three thousand miles away. This. This was what she missed. Without River having to explain, Jasmine knew something was up right away. She sighed. "Vaughn is back. I saw him last night."

"Shit." Jasmine scooped her dark hair back over her shoulder. "Took him long enough. Sarge sent the letter months ago."

"Yeah, still not over that," River responded drily. "Something about a PO box. Guess that's why no one could find him." A jab of pain landed in the center of River's chest, renewing her determination to do what was best. "He really didn't want to be found."

Jasmine was silent for a beat, as if deciding where to start. "What did he say about Marcy?"

The picture on the screen froze, before resuming animation. "I-I think he's still in shock. We didn't get very far before I tried to beat him up in the Kicked Bucket parking lot."

"Oh, Riv." One side of her best friend's mouth lifted. "How'd that feel?"

"Pretty great."

Jasmine sat back in her chair, drinking coffee and waiting.

It was her way—not to push, but to let River speak in her own time. Lord, she appreciated that. They were coming to the reason she had Skyped this morning, for more than their usual social call. There was something she hadn't even told her best friend. Something about the night Vaughn left. And now that the reckoning was coming, she needed someone to remind her she wasn't an awful person. "Jas—"

Sarge walked into the frame...in nothing but a pair of red briefs. River held up both hands to ward off the image, slamming her eyes shut. "No. No, I didn't sign up for this."

"What?" said her brother's sleepy voice. "Oh, hey, Riv." When she looked back at the screen, her rock star brother had made no attempt to cover himself, totally unashamed of his lack of clothing in front of his sister. "I'm still getting used to seeing you blonde again," he said.

"Yeah." She sighed, patting the top of her head, self-consciousness replacing her outrage. She still felt silly for impulse-buying the drug store dye months back, but acknowledging the reason she'd made an effort with her appearance definitely wouldn't help brighten her morning. "Only forty-five minutes and I was right back to my old self."

Ugh. Pity party, table for one. Why was she subjecting Sarge and Jasmine to her melancholy attitude? Having Vaughn back in town was no doubt the catalyst for her doom and gloom this morning—not to mention her nerves—but there was no sense involving her loved ones in problems they could do nothing about. No. She needed to get to work, make money to care for Marcy and add to the college fund that grew a little more every week, and handle Vaughn on her own.

"Sorry to cut this short, but I'm going to be late—"

"River?"

She stood up and whirled around so fast, she upended the plastic stool on which she'd been sitting. Just inside Adeline's small office, filling the doorframe, stood Vaughn, looking freshly showered and…screw it. He was thick and sturdy and sexual. Always had been. "What are you doing here?"

"I've got a better question." He sauntered into the room, muscles flexing with displeasure. "Why are you talking to some dude in his underwear?"

• • •

Vaughn's jealousy slipped over him like a silk net. So familiar and yet he hadn't experienced it in so goddamn long. The emotion had only ever been associated with River, and it appeared that wouldn't change any time soon. If he'd known she would be in the church office, maybe he could have prepared himself to act like a rational human being, but Adeline had directed him to the back—with what he now recalled to be a sly wink—and bam, double whammy. River plus River talking to another man went down his gullet like a handful of spikes.

Her body blocked the computer, so he sidestepped to get a better look, jabbing a finger at the screen. "Who's that?"

"I'm her brother, shit stick." Sarge's voice crackled over the bad connection. "Nice of you to show up."

"Sarge?" The green-eyed monster loosened its strangle hold around Vaughn's neck. And when he peered closer, recognizing a second face from his past, confusion clouded in. "Jasmine Taveras? What are you two doing together? And why aren't you wearing clothes, man?"

"Uh. Call you guys back later," River said quickly, hitting a few buttons and making the screen darken. "They're getting married," she explained quickly, wetting her lips and clearly trying not to look at his chest, which was sending a jolt of heat to his groin area. The girl never could keep from checking him out, and hell, they shared the same affliction. But after a sleepless night where he'd thought of nothing but River's words—*I hate you*—the bags under her eyes took focus.

"Sarge came home for Christmas and kidnapped my best friend. Took her to Los Angeles," she said. "Made her a member of his band." She tightened her ponytail. "What are *you* doing here?"

"Adeline has some of my uncle's things in a box." The man who'd been forced to raise Vaughn after his parents cut out had lived above the town stationary shop, before leaving Hook some time ago. All that was left of Vaughn's upbringing could apparently fit in an Adidas shoebox, which was the description he'd been given by the choir director. "Came to collect the stuff."

"Oh, I'll leave you to it, then." River tried to bypass him, but he blocked her path, a knee-jerk reaction he couldn't help. They were *alone*. His reservoir of missing River had overflowed years back and continued to do so by the minute, flooding his insides. "If you don't have Jasmine, Sarge, or your parents in Hook anymore...who's been helping you, doll?"

"Vaughn." Her eyes flared, then cooled. "It's not for you to worry about."

"I'm trying to be patient with you saying things like that, Riv. I really am." His gut turned over, once, twice. "Will you just talk to me about how it's been...doing this alone? I'm just *hanging* here."

She'd always been a compassionate soul, and that clearly hadn't changed, because his truthful words caused her visible distress. "I have a babysitter—my neighbor, Helen—and she's wonderful. She watches Marcy after nursery school, until I get off at the factory. Sometimes her grandchildren are there, too, and Marcy loves them. They call her Mars Bar."

"Huh," he breathed. He thought of River carrying a little girl up the house's stone pathway, a smile on both of their faces over the nickname, and he barely managed to swallow. "What about when you used to work at the Kicked Bucket?"

"*Used to?*" she echoed. Yeah, okay, he'd said the wrong thing. But he'd die a slow death if she ever set foot in that establishment again, so they'd best get her lack of a night job out in the open. "As far as I know, I'm still on the payroll."

"Guess I'll be making another appearance tonight, then."

Bristling, River stepped into his space, head tilted back, and he gritted his teeth against the urge to incite her further. With a kiss. A kiss that would lead to more. They'd always fucked the hardest when one of them was bent out of shape. He would lay odds on that fact still being truer than a nun swearing on a Bible.

"I didn't look for you, Vaughn. But I know people did, long before my brother sent that letter. Adeline. Duke."

Duke Crawford was his old army friend, who now worked at the local factory, like River. It came as news that he'd been looking for Vaughn, but the pain of River not caring enough to seek him out overshadowed his surprise, as irrational as it was.

"You obviously didn't want to be found," she said. "And I understand. I understand wanting to be free of Hook and… your life here. It wasn't ideal."

She took a long breath, and Vaughn found himself mimicking the action, just to feel in league with her somehow. *Not ideal? Not ideal? I had* you.

"We were young, and we got pregnant," she continued. "It happens all the time. I wouldn't change the outcome, though. And I'm not bringing a man who has a habit of leaving into my daughter's life. You left me for the army. You left me for God knows where."

The axe swung down, even though she hated being an executioner. Vaughn could see it, written all over her, the conflict of regret and determination.

"I won't allow Marcy to get attached then have you pull the rug out. You'd kill her. Same way you killed me."

"River," he wheezed, wet cement pouring down on his head. *I killed her. Fuck.* How could he survive with that knowledge? "I would have come back if I'd known. I'm back now to make this right."

"I don't want your consolation prize. *We* don't want it." Her shoulders sagged as she walked toward the door. "I'm sorry, Vaughn, but there's no place for you here. There hasn't been for a long time."

His insides were scraped raw as the office door shut, sealing him off from River. As if he hadn't done that himself, years ago. *You'd kill her.* Marcy. Was that true? Had coming back to Hook been a huge mistake for River and Marcy? He'd never been good for River, and he still wasn't. Possibly even *worse* now that he'd spent years numbing himself while she busted her ass to raise their child. Was it worth trying to convince River—*and* himself—that he could stay? Or was history doomed to repeat itself?

Hadn't he bailed just like his own parents?

With that ugly thought knocking around his skull, Vaughn reached toward the desk, batting off the top to the Adidas box containing his uncle's possessions. His pulse lurched when he spotted a picture of himself and River right on top, as they'd been when she still attended high school. God, the way she used to look at him. As if a cape were all he needed to be some powerful superhero. The opposite of how she looked at him now.

Did it have to be, though? Maybe he'd never earn back that pure, perfect trust. But even a sliver of that former belief she'd had in him? Fuck, it would make life worth living. To have that trust from his child, too, would be the stuff of dreams. Dreams he'd never been aware of having. Until now. And after so much time devoid of feeling, that hope was addictive.

Vaughn's step was purposeful as he left the office, shoebox wedged in the crook of his elbow.

Chapter Four

Vaughn watched River from across the street, wondering why the hell she was eating lunch by herself. Could have been worse. She could have been sharing a homemade sandwich with a man. As had been proven that morning, jealousy was the kind of emotion that didn't give a damn about rights. On days when coping with memories of being overseas, memories of River, got too thick and bunched up around his neck, sometimes demons crept in. One such demon in particular was the image of her in the arms of another man, almost as if his subconscious wanted to push him that final inch into madness.

Dangerous. Dangerous to think of River as his. When he'd left her crying out for him forty-nine months and four days ago, he'd relinquished any claim on her personal life. A fact that needed remembering.

There were several reasons why he'd left River behind, one of them being his fear he would keep her from reaching the potential she'd been born with. Staying in Hook after her high school graduation, wasting two years attending night classes and working at the factory... Staying in this second rate town *for him*. The guilt had driven him crazy.

He'd joined the army after her twentieth birthday in the hope—which he could see now had been subconscious—that River would see reason and go make a better life in the time he was gone. Go to a real college. Hell, she'd had the grades, the tuition money set aside by her parents. What had been holding her back?

Vaughn. *Him*. A fist-fighting, vehicle-boosting delinquent turned part-time mechanic. Not worth her time. Not even worth her notice. And all that...*all that* had been before he'd come back from overseas with a head full of screams and bomb blasts. Before the army, he'd been beneath River. But after serving, he'd been cancerous.

I'm not bringing a man with a habit of leaving into my daughter's life.

If he wanted the chance to become a father, he would have to backburner his feelings for River. Hell, he had zero business trying to recapture their relationship anyway. None. God, on top of ruining her youth, he'd left her high and dry as an adult. If she allowed him the chance to break the cycle his parents had created, he'd need to be grateful. Wanting more and being denied would be murder.

Unfortunately, the man who'd been compelled closer, always closer, to her in high school—the man who'd dared to touch her magic—felt hollow and restless watching her eat alone.

"Shit," he muttered, climbing out of his truck. From her perch on the hood of her car, River jolted, then grew very still when she saw him approaching—the exact opposite of the circus performance happening live in his stomach. Goddammit, even in her factory jumpsuit, goggle marks on her forehead, she was sunshine breaking through storm clouds. Had it only been a matter of hours since they'd parted ways? "All the popular kids must be sick today for the class president to be eating by herself."

River set her sandwich down on the plastic bag in her lap. Carefully, gently, the way she'd always done everything. Until they got kissing, he silently amended. Nothing careful or gentle about what happened when their mouths met.

Stop fantasizing about something you can't have and never deserved.

"I'm not class president anymore," she said after a beat. "Anyway, I like the quiet."

"You used to hate it."

"No." She shook her head. "I hated it when *you* were quiet. When I couldn't figure out what you would do or say next, or what you were thinking about."

"You." He swallowed, berating himself for the slip but unable to hold everything inside when she—the one who haunted him every moment of the day—was *right there*. "It was always about you."

River shot him a stormy look, before unfolding her legs and sliding off the hood, making it necessary for Vaughn to swallow a groan. Hadn't he taken her once on that hood? *Yes.* He had, but she'd been facing the windshield. *Jesus.* "Why are you here, Vaughn? I already said everything that needed to be said this morning."

Hell if I can stay away. I never could. "I didn't like how lonely you looked sitting here." Based on her startled expression, he'd said way too much. Again. "Just thought I'd give you some company."

A car passed behind them on the street, music blaring through the rolled down windows, while River watched him. "I meant, why *exactly* are you in Hook?" She lifted a hand and let it drop. "Coming back here…what are you hoping to accomplish?"

There was too much history between them. Good, bad,

and ugly. Lying was useless where River was concerned, and with her raising their child alone, the respect he'd already felt toward her had increased tenfold. "I heard you loud and clear this morning. About my leaving. I'll own that. But I'm Marcy's father, and I deserve the chance to meet her." He stepped closer, a ruthless shot of pain spearing him in the chest when she edged away. "On your terms, River. Your terms."

Her nose started to turn red, a sure sign she was getting upset. Lord, he hadn't considered the prospect of her crying. The last time he'd made her cry, forty-nine months' worth of nightmares and cold sweats had been born. *Please not again.*

"What am I supposed to tell her? Who are you?" She blew out a breath. "If I tell her the truth, she'll be crushed when you go away."

When, not *if.* She'd really been stripped of all her faith in him. "I can just be a friend." He would have said anything in that moment to avoid seeing River cry. *Anything.* And it was too soon to let her know he wasn't going any damn where. As soon as he'd left the church this morning, he'd called his employer and given notice.

"A friend," River repeated, her brow furrowing. "I want to say no, but…I can't imagine never knowing her. I hate being the one standing between you and the best part of my life."

"I know that, doll," he managed through his tightening throat. "I know."

She rolled her lips inward, wetting them. "I just need to think about it."

His fingers shook with the need to tuck a stray blonde hair back into her ponytail, so he shoved them into his jeans. "All right. You know where I'm staying."

Blue eyes went wide. "The motel?"

"There's only one in town," Vaughn returned softly, loathing the haunted quality of her voice. "I'm not in our room, though."

"Our room." She sounded distant, her attention on something invisible over his shoulder. "I went back there once, when I was pregnant with Marcy. It sort of...I don't know. I felt you in the room. I assumed you would just *know* about the baby after I'd been there. Isn't that dumb?"

An invisible rope tried to rip his heart out through his mouth. Especially when River seemed to realize what she'd said out loud, both of her cheeks flaming bright pink.

"*No*," he said hoarsely. "No, that wasn't dumb. You've never done anything dumb in your life, except getting hooked up with me."

She gave him that reproving look he remembered so well. The one that had always flipped his self-loathing on its head because at least *River* saw his worth. But it must have been muscle memory or reflex, since it faded from her features just as quickly as it appeared. "I..." She visibly shook herself, moving around to the car's driver side and opening the door. "I have a picture. Of Marcy. That'll have to be enough for now."

Pulse pounding in his ears, Vaughn watched through the windshield as she lifted the console compartment and took something out. When she climbed back out of the car, Vaughn had moved without realizing it to meet her.

And when River placed the photograph in Vaughn's hand, the ground shifted beneath his feet.

• • •

Don't cry. God, whatever you do, don't cry.

This couldn't be the monumental moment she wanted it to be. Maybe if Vaughn had come back to Hook when she was pregnant, or when Marcy had been an infant, River could have allowed this moment, this presenting of a child's image to her father for the first time, to mean something important.

But it was far too late now. She'd wept her tears and pined for Vaughn's return. She'd seen the bottom of despair, and it was a painful, lonesome place.

But, God, Vaughn made it hard not to react with her entire shipwrecked soul. His eyebrows went up, breath hitching once before coming out in a huge rush, fluttering the edges of the picture, in which Marcy was dressed like a pumpkin for Halloween. He shook his head, like maybe until that moment, he hadn't really believed they'd created a tiny human being together.

Vaughn let the picture fall to his thigh, the opposite hand coming up to drag down his open mouth. "Ah, doll. She looks just like you." He tried to clear his throat, but it was obvious from his voice he hadn't succeeded. His boots scuffed on the black pavement as he paced away and returned. "Christ, River. We had a baby?"

His words sent her back to the day she'd gone into labor, the way she'd gotten through the ordeal by imagining him there, substantial and reassuring. Real. "Yes." She had to look away from the gravity in his eyes before it sucked her in. "We *made* a baby." In her periphery, River saw Vaughn lift the photograph again. She knew every detail he took in. Knew that while Marcy took after her, she'd inherited Vaughn's devilish smile. "You can hang on to that. I have to go back—"

Vaughn entered her personal space without warning, bringing River's back up against the car, dropping her pulse into a tumultuous downbeat. His bottomless brown eyes ran over her face, intense, so intense. Which she might have been able to resist, if it weren't for the vulnerability lurking in their depths. "What was it like?" His attention drifted down to the space between them, that regard burning her alive. "Did you...have an easy time, Riv?"

His tortured tone pinned her to the car, rendered her feet incapable of carrying her away. "She was a C-section." A need to ease the pressure in her throat had River trying for levity. "I have an ugly scar now. I'm not your flawless class president anymore."

Vaughn crowded closer. So close she could feel his breath pelting her lips. Had his hand just grazed her hip? "Let me see it."

River's head was too busy spinning to make sense of his request. *He's touching me. He's touching me.* "See what?"

She almost moaned when his knuckle traced down her belly. "Show me the scar." They met eyes when his hand slowly flattened on her stomach, his thumb applying just a bare amount of pressure, but it might as well have been a full body rub the way her senses went crazy, and crazier still when his upper lip grazed hers. "It's too late for me to be there for you. It's so fucking late, doll. But I need to see what you went through. I need to pretend for just a second that I was a part of it."

If for no other reason than to insert an object between Vaughn and her heart, River wedged a hand in at the top of her jumpsuit zipper. With a deep breath, she dragged it down, down, exposing her blue cotton T-shirt, a Giants logo at the center. Vaughn eased back just enough to reach out, his fingers shaking as he gripped the T-shirt's hem. He lifted the material and tugged her jeans' waistband down to reveal the thin red scar running low and horizontal on her abdomen.

His pained sound dotted the air between them.

"It doesn't hurt," she felt compelled to say, but it didn't seem like he heard her because one second he towered over her, and the next, he'd fallen to his knees. "What…"

His mouth landed on top of her belly button, filling the indentation with warm breath. Lips, so familiar and so new at the same time, moved lower—too low—kissing along the scar with painstaking tenderness, left to right. River's legs dipped, her back sliding a few inches down the car door. Had she moaned out loud? Yes…she had. When was the last time someone had touched her? *Really* touched her, skin to skin? Vaughn, ages ago, inside a stale motel room while a cheap clock radio played static-laced Snow Patrol.

She tipped her head forward and found Vaughn watching her intently, with undeniable heat—and something closer to an apology—as his mouth moved higher. His hands, too. They skated up her rib cage to fist beneath her breasts. "Vaughn, stop. You have to stop."

"I'm sorry." He laid his lips against her scar one final time and stood, those devastating hands still beneath her shirt. "I'm sorry for the pain that went into that scar. I'm sorry you did it alone."

Don't come any closer. She needed to say it, but the heat, the physical contact, was decadent after being cold and bereft so long. "I wasn't alone," she whispered. "I had Jasmine…my family—"

"You needed *me*, though." Their foreheads met, and one muscular arm slipped between the small of her back and the car. "You needed me, and I was long gone. I'll never make that up to you." He tugged her up into his big body then pressed her against the car, so securely the vehicle swayed. "Can I comfort you now, Riv? For just a minute?"

Her gaze found his waiting mouth, so sculpted and masculine, a white scar at the right corner, courtesy of a bar fight. "If you think this will comfort me, you're wrong," she breathed, watching as his expression darkened, grew more like she remembered it. Restless. Hungry for her. *Always* hungry.

"You're right. There's nothing comforting about what happens when we touch, is there?" His thumb brushed her nipple, and she jerked between his body and the car, sucking air in between her teeth. "Will you settle for wet and worked up?"

River had no time to respond because Vaughn tilted his head a few degrees, those deep, brown eyes blazing, and went in for the kill. The impact of the kiss didn't occur *just* at her mouth. No, she felt it square in the chest, deep in her midsection, closing in from all sides. Every single component of her being rose like a tiny phoenix and clamored toward the man who'd awakened her once upon a time, each ready to beg for another round. All of that took place with their mouths fused close, *so tight*, but not moving. And when Vaughn's sturdy frame shuddered and he widened his lips along with hers, teasing the tips of their tongues together, her center of gravity tilted and dropped, right along with her belly.

He pulled back. "Your scar is beautiful," he said, his low declaration shimmying through her fingers and toes.

And then he invaded her mouth like he owned it, like he'd never been gone, not for a second—as if they'd been suspended within the kiss for four years, just waiting to proceed. His hand closed around her breast, the opposite arm tightening at her lower back, pulling her against him. They groaned into the contact, thighs shifting in restless, writhing motions against one another, mouths beginning to move with feverish intent.

A jagged warning slashed in River's head when his hips began to roll, one booted foot edging between hers to widen her stance. So he could take her outside, in broad daylight? *Ahhh.* Heat rushed between her legs, preparing, even as common sense attempted to intrude, reminding her a coworker could emerge at any moment. A car could—

Vaughn changed tactics, giving her a gasp-inducing upthrust, elevating her against the car, rocking the vehicle as he growled. "I don't know what to do with this fucking *urge*, Riv." His words were agonized against her swollen mouth. "It's like my body needs to thank yours for bearing our child. Just want to get between those legs and give. *Give.*"

River's vision doubled before everything swooped back together. Reality was unwelcome when her body sang for more touching, more touching from *this specific man*, because apparently her hormones and her heart didn't regularly communicate. And forget common sense—that traitor had taken a vacation. "No. *No*, Vaughn." It took an effort to squirm free of his determined grip, but when she finally managed it, her hand moved of its own accord, cracking against Vaughn's cheek. Any other time, she would have been shocked by her own violence, but anger built with a vengeance, leaving room for nothing else. When she spoke, her voice was whisper-thin. "How dare you kiss me like that?"

"*Riv…*"

She could see the scene play out behind his eyes, although she only knew it from her own point of view: Vaughn, dead-eyed and unfeeling, turning his back on her and walking out, leaving her in the motel room—*their* motel room—where she hadn't moved until the manager booted her out two days later. Not that he knew it. Not that she would tell him. She didn't *need* to. Not with the meaning behind her question hanging in the air like rotten fruit. *How dare you kiss me like that when you left me shattered, without even glancing back over your shoulder?*

He would walk away from their child without looking back, too.

When shame began to filter into his expression, River turned away, walking on shaky legs toward the bumper. "I don't need to be thanked. I don't *want* it either. Being a mother to her has been all the reward I need." She took a deep breath and met his hooded gaze. "But I'll make you a deal."

His throat muscles shifted. "Do I want to hear this?"

She ignored his question, focusing on the dull thump of her heartbeat. "I'll let you meet Marcy. But only if you leave town afterward and don't come back."

Chapter Five

A significant part of Vaughn had hoped the Third Shift, Hook's resident dive bar, would have bitten the dust by now. But no. The scene of countless fistfights—starring him—still hung on by a thread, neon signs flickering in the window. Yeah, he'd thrown so many punches in the place, he'd earned the distinct honor of Hook's first banned customer. That title had been bestowed the year before he'd joined the army, when he'd spent countless nights propped on a creaky stool, attempting to deaden the guilt over keeping River as his girlfriend. Those evenings she'd been taking night classes at the closest junior college, secure in the rightness of her course.

"I'll get my associates degree, just to make Mom and Dad happy. Just until they can see staying in Hook is the right thing. You and me." She reached out and adjusted the heat in his truck, rubbing her hands together for warmth until Vaughn gathered them in his own, performing the task for her. *"They*

met at our age," River continued, blushing with pleasure over the gesture. "They've just forgotten what it's like" — her gaze dipped — "to love someone more than anything in the world."

Vaughn coughed to hide the way his breath whooshed out. "You know I love you, too, doll. That's why I would be right here waitin', not matter what you did, or where you went. To college, to study abroad…" He released her hands in favor of tipping up her chin, trying to impress upon her the sincerity of what he was saying. "I can't let you regret being with me."

Maybe if she went and did those things, she'd finally have no choice but to admit there was more out there for a girl like her. So much more. Everything.

Perceptive as they came, River's shoulders tensed at something she'd read between the lines. Something accurate, if he could only find the willpower to do the right thing for once in his worthless life. "Promise me you won't leave. Promise me you won't ever leave me. Unless you quit loving me," she added, voice barely audible. "I won't stop you then."

His stomach dove to the driver's side foot well. "I promise, Riv."

The painful flashback propelled Vaughn into the Third Shift, where he came to an abrupt halt. Out of necessity — Hook's crown jewel of spilled beer and blood was packed to the gills. Arguments, shouting, and shitty music slapped him in the ears, sounds that would normally grate, but were a welcome muffling of his current thoughts of River. But the bar only saw this large turnout when someone died, retired, or got married, so there was a high likelihood he would be recognized. Meaning he would have to converse, explain where he'd been. And that was something he definitely couldn't stomach after seeing such sadness in River's eyes that afternoon. Best to blow this—

"Don't even fucking *tell* me that's Vaughn De Matteo over there looking like a slapped ass."

Vaughn's hand paused halfway to the door handle, dread and amusement fighting a war under his sternum. He knew that brash, booming voice, and he knew it well. It came from quite possibly the only person in Hook—apart from River—that he would let call him a name without an emergency room visit.

Schooling his features, Vaughn turned from the exit and presented his middle finger. "Ask your mom about my slapped ass."

Duke Crawford threw back his head and laughed, easily drowning out every other sound in the bar, and receiving more than a few eye rolls from the sparse female clientele. The veritable giant wound his way through the crowd toward Vaughn, a bottle of Budweiser looking so at home in his fist it could have been an additional appendage. Now a mechanic at the local factory, Duke had once served alongside Vaughn in the army, and was the only man on the planet Vaughn would consider calling a brother. He was one of the most generous men Vaughn had ever met, but also the type to say *fuck you* for pointing it out.

Vaughn braced himself a second before Duke's massive paw came down on his shoulder. "Well, shit, bro. You don't call, you don't write." Another low, rumbling laugh brought back memories. *The smell of gun oil and heated earth, the feel of the ground shaking.* "How the hell are you?"

Noticing curious eyes flashing toward him, and whispering behind turned backs, Vaughn rubbed a hand over his hair. "Been better. Been worse."

Duke tipped back his beer, regarding Vaughn down the length of the bottle. "You come here to get shit faced? I can help you with that." He jerked his chin toward the crowd over his shoulder. "Everyone's tying one on tonight—might as well join our ranks."

"Any particular reason? Or is it a day ending in *Y*?"

"Still a ball-breaker, huh?" Duke pounded him on the back. "Good. You'll need it if you're sticking around."

Vaughn lifted an eyebrow. "You sound pretty sure I'm here to stay."

Duke started backing toward the packed bar, waving at Vaughn to join him. "You escaped Hook once. Don't think it'll let you get away with it twice."

Vaughn didn't question his friend's sanity for referring to the town as a living entity that decided who stayed and who left. Hell, maybe he was right. Vaughn had never entirely let the town relinquish its hold, had he? When they bellied up to the bar, wedged in between men he identified as factory workers by the grease on their hands, Vaughn cursed under his breath. Of course the bartender that banned him way back when happened to be working tonight. Nothing ever changed in this town.

Except for River. She'd changed, hadn't she? Gotten stronger out of necessity, because he'd left her to fend for herself. Strong enough to resist him physically, which she'd never been able to do before. Maybe it made him an asshole, but her lack of willpower around him had been a source of pride when they'd been together. After that afternoon, one thing seemed clear. She really didn't want him, or need him around. Those weren't just words she'd been saying—they were truths.

"I need something stronger than a beer," Vaughn managed around the strangling sensation in his throat.

"Hearing you loud and clear, soldier." Duke narrowed his eyes when the title made Vaughn flinch, but the mechanic must have correctly interpreted Vaughn's mood, because he let it slide. "How long have you been back?"

"Since yesterday." Vaughn cast a glance at the milling crowd. "Seriously, what's the occasion? Is the pope in town?"

Duke propped an elbow on the bar, and Vaughn swore the damn thing sagged under his weight. "The factory got sold. New owner—some New York fucker in a suit—just waltzed in today and gave a speech from the platform, while we all watched from the floor." He drained his beer and made an *ahhh* sound. "So yeah, I guess you can say there's a new pope in town. They've got the same level of importance around here."

Vaughn was too busy processing the news to laugh at the comparison. The same man had owned the factory since they'd learned to walk. What did the changing of the guard mean for River? "Is he going to close the doors?"

"Only for two weeks—he's going to replace some of the machinery. Wants to 'make it green' whatever the fuck that means. He's bringing along his important clients and their expensive contracts. Plus we all get to keep our jobs." Duke pounded a fist on the bar. "Hence the impromptu party. We all just got two weeks paid vacation."

Relief blanketed Vaughn's alarm just in time for the bartender to reach them. "Fellas, what'll it be—*hey*." Recognition dawned beneath two scraggly gray eyebrows. "You here to cause trouble, De Matteo?"

Vaughn gave a single headshake. "Just here for the whiskey."

The bartender pointed at Duke. "I can ban you just as easily, Crawford. You'll be held responsible for any damages."

Duke straightened from the bar, giving the salty older man an exaggerated salute. "I won't let you down, captain."

Two whiskeys were slid in front of them, the bartender walking away muttering about prodigal sons and insurance policies. Vaughn and Duke gave each other sarcastic, sidelong glances before draining the first halves of their rocks glasses.

From Duke's narrow-eyed scrutiny, it was obvious to Vaughn he had questions, so he set down the whiskey with a sigh. "What?"

"What?" There was enough disbelief and anger in that single word to power the factory. "You just blew out of here without telling anyone where you were going. Not even your uncle—and he's long gone now, too." He rubbed at the back of his neck. "I *looked* for your ass, man. There was, uh… circumstances. You kind of left a little something behind—"

"I know about River and the baby." The words had to travel through a razor blade forest to get out. "That's why I'm back."

"*Fuck*." Duke blew out a gust of breath. "I'm glad I wasn't the one to tell you."

"Yeah." Vaughn drained the remaining whiskey from his glass, battling a fierce impulse to smash the object in his fist. *Failure. You fucking failure.* "I appreciate you trying. I'm going to handle it now."

"Is River aware of that? We know each other's business around here. And it's common knowledge River doesn't even take charity from her brother who, no offense, could buy and sell us both." The humor had returned to the mechanic's voice, but he retained a thread of seriousness. "You know, half this town is in love with her, but everyone's too afraid of you returning from the dead to ask her out. Were those guys right to be cautious?"

Jealousy sent a hot tremor coursing through Vaughn. "If you were one of those guys, we're going to have a problem."

"Nah." Duke winked. "Women are too much damn trouble. Anyway, I never could see her with anyone but your ugly ass."

Vaughn forced his fingers to uncurl, placing his palm flat on the bar. "No, they weren't wrong to leave her alone." His mouth dried up. "Even if I can't have her back, I'd want to inflict pain on every one of them."

Even if a second chance with River *wasn't* a pipe dream, too many ghosts still floated around them. Too much left unsaid or unexplained. Communication had never been one of his skills. Even if he'd stayed, would he have told River about his battle to overcome the flashbacks? The survivor's guilt from his time in Afghanistan? Or, hell…the fateful visit he'd been paid by River's father the afternoon of the day he broke it off with her and left town?

The lie he'd told.

So many secrets and shadows around a relationship that represented clean, white light to him. Ironically, now that he yearned to come clean to River, to tell her everything, she was well out of his reach. His family had been built without him. However, down deep in his bones there was a yearning to care for River and Marcy. To be the missing piece, even if he'd always been a piece that didn't fit anywhere. The puzzle would never truly feel complete without calling River his own again, but he'd take whatever scrap they threw his way and be goddamn grateful.

"She said I could meet Marcy, so long as I get lost afterward. Leave town," Vaughn said, feeling the weight of that decision as if it rested on his own shoulders. "After everything she's been through, I hate to push for more. Jesus, what do I know about being a dad, anyway?"

"You're here. That's a damn fine start." They both rolled their necks, neither of them big on sharing. "You know, if you want to earn some brownie points with River," Duke said, breaking into Vaughn's thoughts. "You could start by preventing her hangover."

Vaughn's head came up. "What?"

Duke gestured with his glass of whiskey toward the back of the Third Shift. "I wasn't kidding when I said we're *all* tying one on."

The crowd parted just enough for Vaughn to catch sight of River's unmistakable blonde hair flipping...as she put away a shot of tequila.

"Christ."

. . .

Oh God. What was she doing here? She should be home, using the unexpected night off to clean the house or finish that novel she'd started reading...when? Last year? She'd just phoned the babysitter to let her know she'd be an extra hour. And that hour's end was fast approaching. According to Helen, she was happily knitting on the couch with Marcy sound asleep upstairs. River never went out unless it was a special occasion, so why did she feel so guilty?

Maybe because drinking tequila was an attempt to get the taste of Vaughn out of her mouth. The kiss still lingered, the intensity of it kicking around in her belly every time she replayed it. Which her wiser self insisted she should *not* be doing. Hence the tequila. If she didn't take a proactive approach in eradicating the new memory, she would relive it all night long—as if thoughts of Vaughn didn't already take up way too much of her consciousness.

I'll let you meet Marcy. But only if you leave town afterward and don't come back.

What would Vaughn decide? And why did regret insist on prodding at her? He'd looked so...*devastated* as she'd walked away.

It made no *sense.* He was the one who'd claimed he'd stopped loving her that night four years ago. She could still hear the toneless, callous manner in which he'd said the words. *I don't feel the same way anymore, Riv. I'm sorry.* And what had come after. The desperate way she'd seduced him, trying to convince him he was wrong. *One more time. Just one more time, and you'll see.*

Nine months later, she'd had Marcy.

Feeling a sudden, bone-deep need to be home, to lay eyes on her daughter, River pushed to her feet—and *swayed*, the room doubling around her.

"*Oh.*"

No sooner had she made the decision to sit down until her head stopped spinning than two big hands closed around her biceps, steadying her. "Hiya, doll."

Vaughn. And with a flash of clarity, River realized the real reason she'd come to the Third Shift, a place she normally avoided like the plague. She'd been hoping to bump into him.

For shame, River. You really are a self-destructive idiot. The sentiment became even more obvious when Vaughn brought her close, his breath ruffling the tiny loose strands at her hairline, igniting a flickering white flame in her belly. "I was jus' on my way out." River frowned over the slur in her speech. "You know what I'm m-mean."

His lips had the nerve to tick up at both ends. "You always were a lightweight."

"We keep arguing. And you keep showing up like nothing happened." A hiccup escaped. "Did you used to do that?"

Vaughn's smile dimmed. "We never used to argue."

"There had to be one," she insisted.

Those big fingers started massaging her biceps, sliding up to perform the same soothing action on her shoulders. *Good Lord.* Why did it have to feel so good? "There was one time," he said after a moment. "You invited me over for dinner at your parents' house, and I didn't show because I knew I'd fuck it up. I *knew*, Riv. So you snuck out when they fell asleep, stormed over to my apartment in the dark—which is how *I* got pissed off—and you ended up getting it doggy style on my kitchen floor." By the end of Vaughn's story, his breathing had graduated to rough drags of air. "That's how we handled our one argument."

The memory of having her jeans yanked down by angry hands, her knees sliding up and back on the linoleum floor until Vaughn got frustrated and lifted her legs up like the handles of a wheelbarrow? The forced visual swiped away a huge portion of the tequila fuzz making River dizzy. Vaughn's gaze had dipped to her breasts, which were still covered by the Giants T-shirt she'd worn to work beneath her coveralls. Although she might as well have been wearing a see-through negligee, based on Vaughn's riveted attention. The hands massaging her shoulders had grown more insistent, gathering material with each movement, until the shirt lifted and exposed her stomach.

River wasn't embarrassed by the scar on her belly by any means, she was proud of it, but not having been a sexual object in so long—which *had* to account for the wicked flare of need—her hands automatically flew up to cover herself, tugging the T-shirt back into place. "I-I need to get home."

"I've had one drink. I'm taking you."

"I'm getting a cab."

"Like hell you are." He picked up the purse she'd almost left behind and tucked it under his arm, somehow maintaining ultimate manliness. "A cab driver can't make sure you get up the stairs without breaking your neck."

"Neither can you," River sputtered, panic beginning to dawn. "You *can't* just—"

"I *can't?*" Vaughn inclined his head. "Aw, doll, you keep uttering that magic phrase, almost like you want me to prove you wrong."

River didn't have a chance to protest that insane notion before Vaughn tucked her up against his side, turned, and began to traverse the crowded bar. Something had changed, though, during the course of their conversation. The Third Shift had gone eerily silent, every patron turned in their direction. Some heads were shaking, other customers looked ready to cheer. But each of them had something in common. They were all recipients of a death glare from River.

"Since when do I glare?" she muttered, led out onto the sidewalk by Vaughn, who had an annoying smile playing around his mouth.

"Since I came back to Hook, I'm guessing."

"That's a pretty good indication you should leave—" River's reproof ended in a gasp when Vaughn scooped her off the ground, settling her on the passenger seat of his truck. With a rueful look, he started to close the door, but leaned in at the last second, pinning River to the seat with sudden, breathtaking concentration.

"I was going to wait to tell you this. But you know me, Riv. I don't live according to what someone else decides is the right schedule. And when I say something, I mean it. Like when I told you we'd wait until you were eighteen to start fucking." Vaughn's tongue skated along his bottom lip, attention falling to her thighs, which crossed of their own accord. "So I'm telling you now, I'm not leaving. Give me a chance to meet her, then watch me show up every day afterward, even if you turn me away. I'll show up and take my beating like a man, day in and day out. But you better get used to me, doll. I'm not budging."

Thank God he stopped there, because River's organs were all bunching together, like some organ support group, rendering her breathless. *When I say something, I mean it.* River didn't doubt him. Growing up in the same town, as they'd eventually gravitated toward one another regardless of their social divide, she'd seen how Vaughn had garnered a reputation as a man of his word, whether it had been a threat or a promise. Such as promising they wouldn't be physical until her eighteenth birthday. Or saying he wouldn't leave Hook unless he stopped loving her. Another vow he'd upheld. And maybe it was selfish—no, it *was* selfish—but with the reminder of Vaughn's staunch truthfulness ringing in her head, she could only remember one thing he'd once said. *I don't feel the same way anymore, Riv.*

To this day, she must have been holding out hope he *had* been lying that night, because the last piece of hope left standing...crumbled, revealing her selfishness. Was sending Vaughn out of Hook best for Marcy? Or best for her brutalized heart? Maybe she couldn't be objective where the father of her child was concerned. But regardless of Vaughn's promise not to leave again, she didn't know if trusting him emotionally would ever be an option. Not when she'd handed over her love and had it returned full of holes.

Still...when Marcy became an adult and asked why she'd never met her father, how would River explain sending him away when there was a chance he'd keep his word?

River tore her gaze away from Vaughn, staring straight through the windshield. "Okay."

"Okay, what?" His voice had turned suspicious.

River forced a smile onto her face, but the corners of her mouth felt weighted. "I'll get used to you, I guess." She wiped a palm on her jeans. "We will."

Vaughn didn't respond for long moments, but River could feel his scrutiny. "Thank you, Riv." *God*, he was standing very still, so still. "I don't understand it. Why do I feel like I just lost here?"

"It's been a long day." She swallowed the fist-sized lump in her throat. "Can you just take me home?"

Chapter Six

I've lost her.

A ridiculous goddamn thought, since he'd lost River forty-nine months and four days earlier. Once upon a time, reading River had been simple as breathing. Back when she'd still been in night school and he'd been nothing more than a part-time grease monkey with no high school diploma. When she'd needed reassurance of his feelings, she'd stop talking and clean something, rearranging trinkets on her bedroom shelves until Vaughn got the picture, snatched the broom out of her hand and gave eye contact, lots of it, until she came back down to earth, where he lived for the sole purpose of being her man.

When River had wanted sex—which had been early and often—she would rotate her hips, just a little, no matter where they were. She would push up on her toes and writhe, so subtle that only he noticed. Hell, he'd come to the conclusion that River herself hadn't been aware of the tempting action. Yeah…that mating dance had gotten her pulled into enclosed spaces all over Hook, although sometimes they didn't even make it that far. That senior year, when she'd turned eighteen halfway through? He'd fucked her an obscene number of times in the alley behind Hook High right after the dismissal bell rang, her textbooks in a scattered heap on the concrete, her slim fingers clinging to the chain link fence, or those long legs dangling around his hips, shaking with the impact of him.

Just one more way he hadn't treated her the way she'd deserved.

Vaughn ground his teeth, casting a sidelong glance at River in the passenger seat. Yeah, he might have grown adept at reading and accommodating River's moods back in the day, but she was sure as shit a mystery now. When he'd pictured River agreeing to his involvement in Marcy's life, there'd been a sense of completion—or homecoming—far-fetched as it sounded, especially after what he'd done. One thing he hadn't expected was the breaking apart of their connection with such a profound snap he'd almost seen it playing out in real time. The familiarity between them had floated away like a colorful balloon, leaving them as strangers in that frozen bubble of time.

Pulling up in front of River's house brought up enough memories to paralyze Vaughn in the driver's seat a moment, but he propelled himself from the truck to help River down. She was still unsteady on her feet in a way that made Vaughn yearn to carry her up the porch steps, but intuition kept his arm in its safe place around her shoulders.

"I have to pay the babysitter," she murmured, before one hand flew to her mouth. "Oh my God. You can't..." His eyebrows went up at her word choice. "Okay...*I* can't have her thinking I'm bringing home a man."

Possessiveness blew into his stomach with the power of a hurricane. "You've never brought a man home before." Not a question. "Jesus, Riv. I *really* don't fucking mind knowing that."

"How exciting for you," she snapped, face turning pink in a way that got his juices flowing like the rapids. "You've seen me home. Thank you. Now, please leave. Tomorrow you can show up without any warning and tease me into another argument."

Vaughn put one hand on the doorjamb and eased closer, tucking stray hair behind her ear, a move natural as inhaling. "Teasing you? Is that what I've been doing?" *I should back off, but she's looking right at my mouth.* "Teasing implies I didn't mean to follow through, and...*ahhh*, Riv, I would've sent you back into that factory with bite marks and a smile if you'd let me."

Her chest lifted and fell on a shudder. "Is that right?"

When had their faces gotten so close? "Don't ask questions when you already know the answer."

Damn, he was overstepping. He should've let River maintain her good reputation with the babysitter, but something about the strong possibility she'd been without sex since they were together...yeah, she'd basically busted the dam holding back his testosterone, sending it flooding into his bloodstream. Not good. *Really* not good when River was half in the bag, and she'd just agreed to allow Vaughn into their lives. Any kind of sexual advance could blow his progress to hell, but Christ, when had he ever been logical in anything River-related?

Hell, though. Maybe he still had the ability to read River somewhat, because she was giving those familiar signs of digging in her heels. Her shoulders were bunched up in the vicinity of her ears, the fingers of her right hand curling into a ball. If he didn't want this time she'd allotted him to be over, he'd better pull back on the instinct to touch and possess... all of her.

Jesus. Pull back, man. Before it's too late. He should leave. Now. But being with River was like standing in the light after four years in a cave. Retreating to his hole without being forced was impossible. "I'll meet you inside."

"What..."

Vaughn winked at River as he backed down the stairs. "You still keep the key under the ugly frog statue?"

"It's not ugly. And you can't—" When Vaughn shook his head at her unfortunate phrasing, she broke off, stomping her foot on the wooden floorboards. "*We* can't," she clarified, those big eyes pleading at him from above. As in, *we can't go inside for the purpose of ripping off one another's clothes.*

"I know, Riv." A wave of regret punched him in the gut. How many times would his decision to leave hurt her all over again? "I won't...touch you again unless you invite me, all right?"

The words had been pried from his mouth by rusted pliers, but they satisfied some of the guilt bubbling in his abdomen. With one final glance at River's slight form, Vaughn continued his journey to the back door, cursing himself for making the promise. Because there would be snowballs in hell before he ever broke another promise to River...no matter how much his body yearned to break all the rules.

• • •

River paid Helen—who seemed to take a month packing away her knitting supplies—and went through her nightly ritual of turning off lights and securing the house. Although, it was much more difficult to accomplish the tasks after a pint of tequila...and with Vaughn watching her from the bottom stair. Grave eyes followed her from the living room to the kitchen, watched as she checked the locks on the windows. She tried not to rush through the process, pushed by her tired brain into making the point that their lives wouldn't be completely altered just because he'd come back to Hook.

In her periphery, she saw him shift positions, obviously uncomfortable, just as he'd always been in the living room of her family home. Her parents might not be there anymore, but her father's disapproval of Vaughn must have lingered, judging from his visible restlessness. She'd once asked her mother why her father held Vaughn in such low regard, and surprisingly, his reputation as a troublemaker was only half responsible. Like many contentious relationships in Hook, the dislike went back a generation—a dispute between *their* fathers, the origin of which River was only partially aware. But she'd known enough to be sure that it had nothing to do with the Vaughn *she'd* known, so she'd never pursued a full explanation.

She didn't know him anymore, though. Or did she?

Maybe it was the alcohol tinkering with her mind, the emotional upheaval of her wayward ex storming back into her life, or a combination thereof, but she experienced the sudden need to knock him off balance, the way he'd done to her by coming home, issuing promises, looking at her the way he used to.

But lying to herself had been River's default of late, so she decided to be honest about the other reason she wanted to throw Vaughn into his own tailspin. Feeling like a desirable woman, being touched and lusted over…it had been too long. He had woken up a wealth of sexual energy in the eighteen-year-old she'd once been, but the hunger for intimacy had been left to cool its heels. Waiting for…what? Her hormones hadn't vanished simply because she'd become a mother. Whether she liked it or not, the way he looked at her was making serious waves in the tide pool she'd managed to keep semi-calm. The difference now being that love wasn't part of the equation. Was there a way she could feed the demands of her body without feeling hurt or used afterward?

Yes…

River's pulse went wild as the idea occurred to her. Not giving herself room to back down, she swayed toward Vaughn, where he'd risen to his feet on the staircase. He held out a big hand, which she took, allowing him to help her to the second floor. The flapping wings in her stomach beat with abandon, and maybe some melancholia when Vaughn remembered exactly which bedroom she slept in, opening the door with an air of authority that turned her on, despite herself. Despite everything.

She watched his Adam's apple rise and plummet as her bed came into view. The same bed in which they'd made love when Vaughn hadn't yet rented his apartment, or when they couldn't afford the motel room or hadn't yet rented his apartment.

His gaze was still burning a hole in her sunny yellow bedspread when he spoke gruffly. "Okay, doll. Got you home safe, but I need to go now." Their fingers slipped apart, Vaughn backing toward the open door. "I'll find you tomorrow."

"Vaughn."

Blunt, impatient fingers attacked his hair. "You should maybe have some Tylenol handy for the morning—"

His advice broke off when she freed her hair of its ponytail holder, shaking it out around her shoulders. The flapping wings in her chest moved lower, lower until every inch of her skin was sensitized, licked by fluttering feather tips. Vaughn's reaction did it—the dropping of his jaw, the liquid quality that stole over his eyes. Desperate to push, to witness more of his desire for her—it felt so *good*—River gripped her T-shirt's hem and lifted it over her head.

He fell into a single step toward River, reaching out for her hips. "If this is an invitation, you know my fucking answer."

She moved out of his reach. "Do you remember the night, about a week before I turned eighteen, when you climbed in through my window?"

"I remember every time like it happened yesterday," he returned hoarsely. "We'd play games. Touching games, even though we shouldn't have. Even though I damn well knew better." Vaughn's hand fell to his fly, showing no gentleness as he handled his bulge, kneading it, lifting it. "Knew those games would only make keeping my cock out of you harder."

Warmth turned the flesh slick between River's thighs, her breath shortening. "Yes, those games," she breathed, pleasure skating through her tummy when Vaughn perused her thinly covered breasts and licked his lips, the image of a man starved. "I'm thinking of the time I asked you to—" She gasped when his gaze drilled into her, forcing her back a step—a step rendered pointless when Vaughn began prowling closer. *Better say the words before he overwhelms you.* "The time you touched yourself in front of me. The time I watched."

"You're asking me if I remember beating off onto your naked body?" He surged forward unexpectedly, fusing his mouth to her ear. "That's not something a man forgets. Especially not when the girl gets off on it." When she sucked in a breath, Vaughn laughed against the flesh of her neck. "You think I didn't notice? Your orgasms were my *life*. I knew what they looked like, what made them happen fast, slow, hard, easy. I called each of them by name. I was their *best friend*."

River's equilibrium teetered, making her wonder if she was still in a drunken stupor after all. Or maybe she'd been overly ambitious thinking she could handle Vaughn's fierce sexuality.

No. She couldn't show any weakness or evidence of intimidation. There was no going back. "I want you to do it again."

One powerful arm was around her lower back, yanking her into his warmth before she finished the request. Poised on her toes, she was held immobile as Vaughn groaned against her neck, into her hair. "So this is how I die, huh?" His Jersey accent was so thick now, she could've plucked it out of the air. "You're not inviting me to touch you? You're inviting me to *not* touch you?"

"Yes," River managed, trying not to be obvious about inhaling his scent. "You'll only be touching yourself."

"Tell me why, first." His huge frame was heaving with the effort to breathe. "I think I have the right to know that much before I stroke myself for your entertainment."

River closed her eyes and four years fell away. Vaughn was once more the young man who ruled her every thought, her body, her mind. And she was a girl who hadn't discovered her first heartache yet. Reality was right there, hovering in the background, but she pushed it away, determined to take what her body had been crying out for. In the process of letting those years melt away—just for a short time—honesty rippled out, the way it might have from a bright-eyed River, whose heart was still intact. "I…" She curled her fingers in his shirt. "I just need to feel sexy."

Her back landed on the bed so fast she bounced, only recovering from her shock when Vaughn's fingers began making quick work of her jeans, unbuttoning, jerking the zipper down, and shucking the denim across the room. "River, you almost had me coming in my pants earlier, dressed in a pair of baggy coveralls." His attention raked her, starting at her neck and ending at the juncture of her thighs. "That's not what you're wearing now, though, is it? You want to recreate a memory, we're going to do it right. That means your tits need to be on display. We on the same page?"

What had she gotten herself into here? She remembered being with Vaughn…but she hadn't *remembered* remembered. When given the green light, he charged like a bull, mowing down everything in his path to get to her. This was what she'd wanted, though. Painful longing streaked down her middle, hitting its target and sending her fumbling for the front clasp of her bra. "My underwear—"

"Has to stay on," Vaughn finished for her. He climbed onto the bed and straddled her waist, stealing her remaining reservations with his size, his commanding energy. With determined but methodical movements, he jerked his leather belt through the loops of his jeans. "You think I don't remember the one rule we made, doll? A man doesn't forget being kept away from virgin pussy by a little strip of material. Knowing a girl loves the sight of his dripping prick before she even knows what it's capable of." He growled above her. "Uh uh, Riv. I didn't forget that. It might be the last thought that runs through my head when I leave this world."

River's hands lost their function and fell to the side, taking her sheer bra along with them. She barely registered the exposing of her own breasts until Vaughn reacted. He fell forward, bracing a hand on the headboard above her head at the last minute, the other hand fighting with his zipper. As she watched in riotous anticipation, Vaughn drew out his erection, already stroking the length of flesh with a guttural groan.

"Fuck, you're even better than I remember." He heaved the words, close enough to paint her mostly naked body with hot breath, tightening her nipples into straining peaks, shifting the flyaway strands of hair on her forehead. "I've been inside that body. I've pleasured that body. Haven't I, Riv?"

Tearing her attention away from the fist pumping up and down on thick, ruddy flesh was near impossible, but the note of distress in Vaughn's voice attracted her like a bee to honey. *Soothe. Correct.* It was like falling back into a rhythm she'd been born to play. "Yes, you were inside me…pleasured me."

He exhaled on a shudder, that hand moving, squeezing, faster, *faster*. "I'm sorry," he groaned. "I've jerked so much come out of my dick thinking of you, I should be ashamed of myself. And I didn't even know you'd gotten sweeter." Those brown eyes had gone deep, almost black, staring down at River, right through her. "I...are you really underneath me right now? Jesus, I can't breathe."

It took her a moment to realize Vaughn wasn't just rambling in that dirty way she'd never stopped craving. No, his breathing was labored, sweat trickling down the sides of his handsome face. Overheated? That was all River's lust-coated brain could conjure up, so she pushed up on one elbow, reaching for the hem of his T-shirt. "M-maybe you should take this off."

She'd only lifted the garment past his belly button, catching just a hint of blue ink on Vaughn's skin—a new tattoo?—before his voice stopped her dead. "*No.*" Seeing that he'd startled her into dropping the hem, he reached for her wrist, rubbing a comforting circle onto her skin with his thumb. "No, it's not the shirt. It's *you*, okay?" His lids dropped into slits. "Christ. Maybe I'm too fucked up for this."

All she heard from Vaughn's mouth was *it's you*, and insecurities dog piled on top of one another, cutting off her air. *I don't feel the same way anymore, River.* God, was he doing this out of guilt in some attempt to apologize? She shot up into a sitting position, attempting to slide her legs toward her chest, away from Vaughn, but his face went tight with alarm, and she found herself pinned to the bed. Both of them were breathing wildly into the sliver of space separating their faces.

"Get off me," she whispered.

Vaughn's head dipped forward, a tortured sound fleeing his lips. "No."

Chapter Seven

Something fucked up was afoot. Most of it was him. Almost *all* of it, actually. Looking down at River while taking his pleasure had felt beyond wrong. So damn *wrong*. He'd torn them apart—hurt this beautiful creature—and the last thing he deserved was an up close and personal peep show while he got his rocks off. Self-disgust came part and parcel with self-pleasure in his world, but not like this. He'd sensed the wrongness in the center of his chest, like a hunting knife twisting.

And now…now, River had that look. One he recognized well. If she were still that twenty-year-old girl, he would say it meant she was insecure about his feelings. But that ship had sailed and he'd been at the helm. Still, nothing would stop him trying to repair it.

Without hesitation, Vaughn kicked into fix-it mode, grasping the sides of her face, forcing eye contact, focused on the patchwork quilt being stitched together inside her head. Not an easy feat considering his hard cock was now wedged up against her cotton panties, like a man begging entry to the only home he'd ever known.

"Stop looking off to the side," he grated. "You know damn well I'll stay like this all night."

"I don't know anything about you anymore," she said through her teeth.

Those words had the effect of a cheese grater rubbing up the back of his spine. "I'm the same man." *Only a shit ton lonelier and only half complete.*

There she went, trying to evade his gaze again, so he pressed their foreheads together, keeping her head still on the pillow. A hint of challenge sparked in her baby blues, and he almost howled with relief. "The same man wouldn't have stopped halfway through what we were doing," she said.

"No, you're right about that. One hundred percent." Sinking his teeth into his bottom lip, Vaughn rolled their lower bodies together, watched her eyes go glassy. "Let me try again. I'm the same man with a different perspective."

"After you explain that nonsense, will you leave?"

He kissed her forehead so she wouldn't see his smile, chock-full of pain though it was. "River…"

Knowing he better not fuck up again tonight, he searched for the right words, even though speaking his thoughts out loud had never been his strong suit. And yeah, he rocked himself up against her pussy while he searched his brain, because *Jesus*, she was so *warm*. Probably slick into her panties, too.

Think. Or just tell the truth, asshole. "Men don't always know what their thoughts mean. Especially me. Not all the way. But I know I felt selfish stroking while you watched. And I've been selfish enough where you're concerned, doll." Another, quicker, punch of his hips, which kicked a gasp up her throat. "It's like, I never expected to have you so close again, and I was wasting it when I really needed to…give you the experience I was giving myself."

Sometime during his speech, he had released the sides of River's face, lifting her hands toward the headboard. The softening of her expression told Vaughn it was safe to release her eyes, and he dragged his attention down between their bodies to the naughty tits poking into his shirt. God, he wanted to feel them slide through his chest hair, but if he took his shirt off, there would be more questions tonight than he could handle.

"Let me get the taste of that pussy on my tongue," he rasped into her neck. "That's what I needed. Fuck, Riv, I couldn't breathe around how bad I want to eat you. Still can't. I felt that little rosebud through my pants today—up against your car—and I'm a sick man now. Am I imagining how bad it needs me?"

River jolted, her body arching underneath him, ripping a growl from his lips. "*Vaughn…*"

Taking a chance, he let his hands travel down the bed to hook beneath her knees. "Did you forget how filthy I am?"

"I must have—"

She broke off on a moan when he yanked up her legs, keeping them just an inch away from his hips on either side. "Say yes, huh, doll?" He slipped his tongue back and forth on his lower lip, watching River's gaze go smoky. "My mouth needs some of this tight kitty." He bucked against her twice. "Don't keep them apart."

"Okay, yes. *Yes*." She slapped a hand over her mouth, proving she did remember what it was like having him between her thighs.

"Good girl," he murmured, sliding his open mouth through the valley of her knockout tits on his way down, down. When he reached the perfect notch of River's legs, nothing could stop him from pressing his face against the sweetness, breathing against the hindering cotton, kneading her calf muscles where he held them aloft. "Remember me?"

he asked, fastening his panting mouth over the spot where her clit was, bathing the material with a lick. "I remember you. The hours of happiness you gave me. The misery you put me through. You were the church I prayed at on Sundays, weren't you? You were *my* Virgin Mary."

River's fingers tangled in his hair, sending some form of sexual heroin through his veins. "Little l-less talking, *please*."

Vaughn's smile was wicked as he glided the panties down her elevated thighs, past her ankles and down to the floor, revealing his only chance at deliverance. "*Oh Jesus*." He fell into her, lapping like a thirsty beggar, until he heard River's hand slap back over her mouth and a muffled scream, the sound like diesel fuel being pumped into his tank. "Still so bare down here. Like your body doesn't want to hide anything from me." His thumb buffed her clit, up and back. "You have no idea what a fucking deviant I felt like, waiting, *waiting* for eighteen…then taking your underwear off and finding you so bare. It was wrong how hard it got me, Riv." He gripped his prick and started to jerk himself off. "But I've never been as rocked up as I am right now, knowing I'm getting the woman as well as the girl."

"Please," came the distorted cry from above, her knees falling open in a familiar signal that she was nearing the end of her patience. God knew he loved getting her halfway there with his dirty speech, but he also knew those fingers in his hair would grow abusive if he delayed any longer.

"Coming, doll."

Vaughn secured River's lower body against the bed, both heels pressed into his shoulders—God bless her flexibility— and *fuck*, he just feasted. Thumbs pressing into her hipbones, he sank into the perfection of her taste. Lightness carried the top of his head up to the ceiling, the melody of her cries playing in his head like a symphony. He alternated between flicking his tongue against her clit and suckling the tiny bud, his middle finger working in and out of her. Beating off with the opposite fist was infinitely more satisfying than how they'd started out, because it was about River, too. About both of them.

Christ, when she'd accidentally implied there had been no other men since him? She'd meant it. He couldn't add his index finger to the banging of her pussy without her hips jerking on the bed, a startled cry from the pillows. Would she let him press his aching cock inside her right now? Maybe. Maybe, but he wouldn't try. Wouldn't claim what he hadn't earned. What he didn't deserve. Not unless she said the words, because then he'd be lost in the fever to please.

And then River's hips and thighs started to tremble on the bed, and Vaughn couldn't think any more. His mouth turned punishing on her clit, lips pressing around the swollen nub, tongue giving it hell and heaven at once, both fingers pressed up into her, a privilege his dick cried out for a second later. His growl of bliss was released against River's flesh, ropes of male fluid soiling River's bedclothes. She followed him into oblivion seconds later, her gorgeous body twisting on the bed, fingers clawing at the comforter, giving his ears the pleasure of hearing her clearly, without the barrier of her hand.

"Vaughn…*yes.* Oh God. *Vaughn.*"

His eyes rolled to the back of his head, the pleasure of hearing River cry out his name almost as intense as the orgasm he'd just lived through. When her body went limp, he crawled over her, admiring the flush of her belly and tits as he ascended, dropping kisses in the rosiest spots. "Beautiful," he murmured, humbled. "Beautiful, beautiful…"

Finally, he reached River's dazed expression…which was already beginning to transform with *oh-shit-what's-next.* Yeah, he got that—real fucking well—even if it hurt like a slug in the gut. So even though the pressure in his throat begged him to push a little further, attempt to stay the night and hold the girl who'd been under his skin for over a decade, he knew better than to press his luck. He'd actually gotten to touch *River* tonight, see to her needs. A week ago, he'd never thought it a possibility.

Don't be greedy.

"Can I see you tomorrow?"

Discerning blue eyes searched his face. "No." She sat up and turned her back, killing him on the spot. But a squaring of her shoulders and a soft smile back at Vaughn resuscitated him. "You can see…us."

"Thank you," he whispered, after a pause that might have gone on a full hour, courtesy of his heart lodging in his mouth. Climbing off the bed and dressing was almost impossible when his instincts demanded he smother River in a hug, and tuck her into his body for the remainder of the night, but he managed to hold back, reminding himself that pushing could damage whatever fragile connection they might be building here, against all odds. With a steadying breath, Vaughn finished pulling on his jeans and went to the window.

"You can go out the front door," she murmured from the bed, a lilt of amusement in her tone.

He winked at her. "Once more for old time's sake."

Right away, he wished he could snatch back the finality of that phrase. They were seeing each other tomorrow. Incredible, but true. And not just each other, but…their *child*. He would battle like a gladiator to make sure nothing about his family *ever* felt final. And suddenly, he knew exactly where to start. When he jumped down into the front yard, there was hope in his chest for the first time since he'd laid eyes on River.

Chapter Eight

River bounded through the hallway of Hook High, ignoring the sarcastic comments from most of her friends—except for Jasmine, who encouraged her with a knowing smile—and burst through the front door into the concrete quad. Inside her chest, a pounding started, so heavy, so extreme, so erratic, she wondered how her body sustained it. Where was Vaughn? Where? He would sustain it for her.

She spun on a heel toward the south end of campus, hitching her book bag higher on her shoulder as she started to jog. The familiar purr of an engine moved the pounding in her rib cage lower on a thrumming slide of new, feminine awareness. She skidded to a halt when she saw Vaughn leaning up against the side of his truck, unmoving and hidden behind sunglasses. She had to give herself a moment, simply so she would survive the impact. God, oh God. He was so hot. She couldn't stand it. Couldn't stand the way he touched her, spoke her name with such...weight. She also couldn't stand to be away from him. Even the school day was unbearable now.

Finally, she got her feet moving again, eating up the stupid distance between them. Vaughn didn't move until she was almost upon him, stepping away from the truck to catch River up in his arms, his ever-present smirk in place. "Hiya, doll."

Her boyfriend swapped their positions, pushing her bottom up against the passenger side door, studying her face with something like confused elation before bringing their mouths together for a groaning kiss.

"What'd I do to earn you, huh?" He tugged on River's blonde ponytail. "Nothin'. That's what."

She squirmed between the truck and Vaughn's rock hard body, a thrill speeding through her belly when she encountered his swelling erection. "Maybe I need to do something to earn you. Did you ever think of that?" Another suggestive squirm had her boyfriend's jaw going slack. "Take me somewhere. Anywhere."

"River, I—" How could his attitude go from aroused to frustrated so fast? "You should be off with your friends. Drinking…milkshakes or something. Studying. Every day can't be about me finding the most convenient place to lift your skirt up and fuck you."

Just hearing the forbidden word on his mouth was enough to cause the now-familiar dampness to spread between her thighs, her lips popping open on a puff of breath. "If you didn't want to….t-take me, you wouldn't be here," River whispered. "And it's more than that. I'm here for what happens after, too. The talking…and holding. Us." She swallowed hard. "Aren't you?"

"Yes," he hissed, before attacking her mouth with a kiss full of fury. "Don't ever ask me that again."

"Yo, De Matteo," a male voice called behind Vaughn. A voice River recognized as one of Vaughn's ex-classmates who now worked as an assistant varsity football coach. "Hands off the students."

Lines formed around Vaughn's mouth, his hands turning

to fists and pounding against the truck. River knew from experience what was coming, so she wrapped her arms tight around his vibrating form and held fast. "Just ignore him. Just—"

When the coach spoke again, he was close enough that only River and Vaughn heard. "How long before she's a pregnant dropout, De Matteo?" He clucked his tongue. "Misery loves company, right?"

She saw the bolt of shame shoot across Vaughn's expression, but it gave way to rage almost immediately. It took two security guards and three senior students to pull Vaughn off the coach that afternoon, while River wept on the sidewalk. When he walked out of jail a week later, once the charges were dropped, he looked disappointed to see River waiting for him, almost as though he wanted to turn around and walk back into jail. Sometimes she still dreamed about that look.

Having an unexpected two weeks off sounded amazing on the surface, but River had been moving without ceasing for so long, the inactivity left her staring off into space…a lot. It certainly was not because of the earth-shaking orgasm she'd been delivered from her long lost, heartbreaker ex-boyfriend's tongue the night before. Or the growly sentiments he'd issued straight to her vagina. *Remember me?*

Oh, heck yeah. Both River *and* her vagina remembered Vaughn's skill set very well. But there had been a difference in him last night…a maturity so different from the brooding young man with the hair trigger temper. Back when they were essentially kids transitioning into adulthood, Vaughn had been a closed book. Last night, he'd shown her, at least, that maybe he was capable of sharing the first couple of chapters. Whereas he'd once been given to occasional bouts of intensity before returning to quiet, frustrating watchfulness, in the heat of the moment last night, he'd been honest with her. That was...new, even if his exact thoughts remained mysterious. Elusive.

Perhaps she was wrong to feel encouraged by what seemed like a changing tide. Maybe the new honesty in Vaughn had begun their final night together when he'd walked out. Left town. She'd forced him to be honest with himself and admit she wasn't what he wanted.

It was possible he'd returned to town solely because the man he'd become didn't shirk his responsibilities—meaning Marcy. And if that was the case, she needed to follow his example and be mature enough to allow it. Starting tonight, when she would invite him over to dinner.

When Marcy nudged River's elbow, she realized she'd been staring into space, leaving her daughter to color the entire Sesame Street scene alone. "Mom*my*, color with me."

Mother's guilt poking her in the gut, River selected a yellow crayon and began to color in Big Bird. They were killing time until mid-morning, when the other kids would start showing up at the local park. Their breakfast dishes were still on the table, which was unusual, since the morning rush had become the household norm. When she'd told Marcy she would be home for two weeks, her daughter's face had lit up enough to make River realize how much she'd been missed. She was looking forward to spending two weeks smothering Marcy with love. "Hey, kiddo. We're having a friend over for dinner tonight."

Marcy looked up from her task, face hopeful. "Jasmine and Uncle Sarge?"

"No." River threaded her fingers through Marcy's blonde hair. "But I miss them, too. They'll come for a visit as soon as the band gets a break."

Her daughter hummed an acknowledgment and resumed

coloring, only to stop again. "What friend is coming?"

Lord, it felt like she'd swallowed a beanbag. She hadn't rehearsed an explanation, never having expected to make one. "His name is Vaughn. He went to school with mommy. Back when we were young."

Which was true. Vaughn had attended Hook High until the beginning of his senior year, when River had been a sophomore. She often wondered if they'd started dating *before* he'd dropped out, if maybe their relationship would have prevented him from making that decision. No way of knowing. No way of being sure of *anything* concerning Vaughn, which is what had her hedging her bet now. "He's just coming for a little while, Marcy. Okay? Not a long time."

"Okay." Marcy's nose wrinkled, already disregarding the subtle warning, but hopefully retaining it somewhere. "When can *I* go to the big school, Mommy?"

"Soon." She smiled, knowing her daughter referred to the big, brick structure that housed Hook High, which they passed frequently in the car. "You'll love it, just like I did."

The words from her own mouth made River's smile fade. She *had* enjoyed school, even night school at the junior college—loved the challenge, the twinkle in her belly when something finally made sense, or she read a particularly relatable piece of literature. She wouldn't trade a college experience for Marcy—not a chance—but she could admit to a tiny background wish to go back someday.

The phone rang in the kitchen, and River stood to go answer. "Hello?"

"Riv."

Her father's curt voice never failed to make her stand up straighter, but love shot an arrow to her heart at the same time. "Hey, Dad. What's up?"

"Not too much. Your mother and I just came back from our walk." His heaved breath echoed down the line.

"Retirement is boring as shit."

Laughing, River leaned back against the kitchen wall. "Only if you let it be. Maybe you should finally give in and go to salsa dancing lessons with Mom."

"Why? Is it snowing in hell?"

Their mutual laughter faded into a silent stretch that made River frown. "Is everything else okay?"

"Yeah. Yeah…" Familiar footsteps paced in the background. "Heard from a buddy yesterday who said De Matteo was back in Hook."

A wrench fell down her windpipe. "Wow. I guess distance doesn't get you free of the gossip mill." She lifted a hand to circle her throat. "Yes, Vaughn is back."

Another stretch of unnerving quiet. "I assume he knows Marcy is his?" Her father scoffed. "I hope he doesn't expect some tearful reunion. Not after what he did."

Not for the first time in her life, River was polarized by the unfair hostility her father exhibited toward Vaughn. Sure, he'd been a troubled young man, but until their final evening together, he'd never done anything to harm her. Quite the opposite. A majority of the time, he'd been sweet and protective, making sure she didn't skip school, bringing her home before her curfew, no matter how much she protested. Whatever animosity had existed between Vaughn's father and her own, it had no bearing on the here and now. She refused to give it credence by asking for the details and creating a forum for her dad to tear down Vaughn. For better or worse, he was the father of her child. "I…don't know what he expects." Okay, not entirely true. His exact intentions weren't clear yet, although he'd been adamant about remaining in Jersey. "But it'll be up to me if he gets what he came for. Okay?"

Since childhood, whenever she showed any kind of backbone to her father, he shut down and didn't revisit the issue until he'd worked out an entirely new tactic, a memory that had River narrowing her eyes.

"I have to go, Dad. Maybe call me over the weekend?"

He cleared his throat. "Sure, Riv. Talk soon."

When she hung up the phone, she stared at the receiver for a full minute, trying to decipher the odd note of... apprehension in her father's voice.

"Mommy!"

River's sigh slipped into a smile. No time to think about it now. She had a play date with her daughter to attend.

Chapter Nine

Vaughn had almost reached the factory door when his cell phone went off in his back pocket. The display showed a number with a Hook area code, so it had to be either River or Duke calling him, both of whom he'd given his number the night before. And damn, the way his blood started pumping told him exactly who he needed it to be. *River.* No damn contest.

Jesus Christ, he'd been a walking hard-on since last night. Not since those two years of abstaining until River reached womanhood had he been this hot to fuck. River. *Always*, only River. He'd woken up in agony, jerking his hips up and back against a scratchy motel pillow, like an animal during mating season. His hand hadn't even been required to relieve the worst of his arousal. Oh no, he'd simply gripped the hollow wooden headboard and accelerated his lewd thrusts, picturing River with her legs spread…and he'd popped right off, shouting down at the mattress. Yeah, considering the state in which he'd left the bed sheets, he probably wouldn't be making friends with the motel maids any time soon.

He'd spent his drive to the factory reminding himself—
around ninety-eight times—that anything physical between
him and River would be on *her* terms. No climbing in through
her bedroom window when he needed to feel her beneath
him naked, to take her down like a starved predator. No.
Remaining focused on his goal was more important now
than ever. *Helping* River. Making up for leaving her a single
mother. If she allowed him into her life as a co-parent, it
would be more than he deserved.

It took several calming breaths before he trusted himself
to answer the phone, but the simple hope she'd be on the
other end made him sound like a goddamn sexual deviant.
"Riv?"

He heard a slow breath that he swore feathered his ear.
"Yeah, it's me."

Warm syrup coated his insides, sliding down nice and
easy. "Hiya, doll," he murmured. "Been a while since you
called me."

"Been a while since I had a reason."

Ouch. Apparently going down on River hadn't been the
remedy to all of their problems. Fair enough. Just meant he
needed to work harder, which was what put him at Hook's
main source of employment so early in the morning. Vaughn
gave a low whistle. "De Matteo takes one on the chin."

He thought he heard a muffled laugh on the opposite end
of the line, followed by a slow breath. "I'm calling to invite
you to dinner tonight."

Vaughn slapped the phone to his chest and mouthed
a *hallelujah* up toward the gray New Jersey sky. When he
finally returned the phone to his mouth, River was issuing
a warning about putting too many Cheerios in his mouth at
once. "Wha—"

"One at a time, Marcy," she repeated twice.

"—kay, I *am*," said a voice he could only describe as

pipsqueak-esqe. And just about everything inside Vaughn seized up, rendering him immobile on the sidewalk outside the factory. He closed his eyes and listened to the sounds of a spoon hitting a bowl, a giggle following fast on its heels, and River's warm laugh. The sounds of home. Amazing that he could recognize them at all, considering he'd never had one. Crashing on an uncle's couch, waiting for his parents to return while knowing full well, even at age ten, they were long gone? Yeah, that wasn't home. That was hell. Everything now drifting down the line, curling into his ear, was a heaven he'd never had the balls to wish for. Funny how a man's perspective could change after realizing there were worse places than hell. There was living without River.

On cue, her voice found him. "Vaughn, are you there?"

"I'm here." He cleared his throat. "What time tonight?"

"Marcy eats early, so around five, five-thirty," she responded, her voice getting lighter, elusive like smoke.

Vaughn could practically feel River second-guessing herself, so he rushed to end the call before that could happen, even though he could have spent the entire day listening to the nuances in her tone. "I'll be there," he said gruffly. "Thanks, Riv."

"Wait." Time suspended itself as he waited for River to continue. "Last night...we got carried away. This...if we're going to do this right, it needs to be about Marcy, okay? Not us."

"You're telling me to keep my hands off you."

A beat passed, giving him hope, despite her answer. "Yes."

It was no less than he'd expected, but being cast into purgatory smarted nonetheless. But no way would he argue. Not with his family at stake. "See you tonight."

Vaughn hung up before River could hammer home her new, unfortunate dictate, and stomped toward the factory entrance, his boots kicking up work dust thanks to the surrounding construction vehicles. Shit. It appeared the factory's new owner wasn't wasting any time making changes. The graffiti-stained, cinderblock wall that had surrounded the factory since Vaughn's earliest memory had been bulldozed, a tasteful waist-level brick barrier already being constructed. New pathways had already been marked, waiting for concrete to fill them. The place already looked less like a prison and more like an office building.

Nodding with approval, Vaughn continued toward the entrance, fairly certain he would find the fancy new owner inside, being that a sleek 2016 Mercedes was parked along the curb. Definitely not a vehicle that belonged within Hook town limits, let alone to any of its residents. Turned out he was right. Just inside the door, a man whose three-piece suit was more appropriate for a corporate board meeting than a construction site stood conversing with a guy sporting a hard hat, going over plans.

Without pausing his stern instructions, three-piece suit gave Vaughn a bored glance over his shoulder—like some kind of overindulged king—and went back to his low conversation, giving Vaughn a moment to size the other man up. Built like a hockey player, but with none of the loose, easy-going energy, the new factory owner wasn't what Vaughn imagined someone might find approachable. Kind of reminded Vaughn of a pissed off lion, actually. And yeah, his observations of the man's appearance were influenced by River eventually being in the man's orbit.

Three Piece didn't address him until a full minute later, once he'd finished issuing dictates to Hard Hat. "Can I assist you with something?" He swept Vaughn with a cool glance. "Perhaps directions to the local watering hole?"

Once upon a time, Vaughn would have already stuffed that expensive tie down the asshole's throat, but he had too much at stake. He only fought for things that mattered now, and this potential job was one of them. "The bar doesn't open this early." Vaughn crossed his arms, leaning back against the wall with a grin. "And trust me, I already know right where it is."

Three Piece rolled up the plans he'd been perusing with precise twists of his cuff-linked wrists. "I find this news unsurprising."

"Why?" Vaughn tilted his head, posing the question out of curiosity more than anything else. "Because I'm dressed to work, instead of ordering other people to do it for me?"

Hard Hat took that cue to leave, slipping out through the entrance, muttering about getting an early start. "Why are you here?" Three Piece asked, voice laced with impatience. "I've guaranteed everyone that their jobs are safe, which I assure you was not a condition of the sale."

"Purely out of the goodness of your heart, huh?"

Three Piece spread his hands in the form of an answer. "I'm due at a meeting."

Vaughn nodded and pushed off the wall. "Sounds good." He turned in a circle, making note of the shiny new machinery, still wrapped with industrial plastic and cardboard. "I'll just be here, determining the street value of all this sweet new gear."

"Excuse me?"

Vaughn dipped his chin toward the entrance. "Who's guarding this place? I just waltzed right in. I get the accessible vibe you're going for—this place has looked like a death trap for too long—but there was a good reason for that cinderblock wall, man."

Three Piece tapped the rolled up plan against his thigh. *Tap, tap, tap.* "I've thoroughly researched the town of Hook. It's low income, yes, but there's not a high rate of crime."

"Sure, but what about one town over. And two towns past that?" Vaughn rapped his knuckles on one of the new massive steel machines. "These renovations won't go unnoticed. You're clearly upgrading technology, too, which means computers—"

"Sounds to me like you're the one I should keep an eye on."

Vaughn shrugged. "Maybe once upon a time. Not now." The back of his neck tightened. "One of your employees means everything to me, and I'd like the opportunity to make sure her livelihood—and she—are protected."

Three Piece narrowed his eyes at that, finally showing a spark of humanity, and easing the pressure in Vaughn's chest. Jesus, job interviews were not his thing, and this one was beyond unconventional. "What credentials do you have?"

"A two-year tour with the Army." Vaughn tugged his wallet out of his back pocket, holding out his Army-issued identification. "I've been working in Baltimore since then, doing private security for visiting business partners and their families. Even upgraded a few local industrial plants—ones like this—to keep the owner's assets protected."

After a small hesitation, Three Piece took the offered identification card, scanning it from beneath heavy eyelids. "If one of my employees means everything to you, what were you doing in Baltimore?"

None of your fucking business, sat right on the tip of Vaughn's tongue, but he swallowed his natural defensiveness, forcing a smile onto his face. "Haven't you ever tried to do the right thing and found out it was wrong?"

"Can't say that I have," Three Piece answered briskly. "I assume you had some type of plan beyond walking in here and insulting my lack of security?"

There's my opening. "Look, one person in Hook knows something, everyone knows it. Already there's word you're taking on bigger contracts, producing more lucrative items. No more license plates or plastic garbage. Maybe no one has had an interest in lifting the merchandise, but that's going to change." He waited for that to sink in. "You need night guards.

Regular patrols. A sophisticated alarm system, surveillance around the perimeter...all of which will lower your cost of liability insurance—"

"Monday morning." Three Piece handed him back the identification. "Bring me your ideas on paper, cost analysis included. I'm late now."

Vaughn nodded once and stepped back. "Can't have that, can we? We'll talk Monday." He stuck out his hand. "Vaughn De Matteo."

"Yes, I read your identification." With a stiff shoulder roll, the other man shook his hand. "Renner Bastion. Please don't show up here in ripped jeans again. I'm not in the habit of hiring men who look like they've been accosted in an alley."

"Welcome to Hook."

Chapter Ten

When the doorbell rang, signaling Vaughn's arrival, River was on the verge of dumping the spaghetti into the trash, turning off the lights, and hiding in the cupboard. That plan would have backfired, unfortunately, considering that Marcy's caterwauling could probably be heard down the block. This state of domestic chaos was not the image she'd planned on projecting. Oh no. She'd actually envisioned herself answering the door in high heels and an unsoiled apron, hair twisted and coiffed, like some modern day June Cleaver, all while Marcy honed her grasp of phonics in the living room. Quietly.

Ha!

The reality of the witching hour—also known as the period of time approaching dinner and bedtime—painted quite a different portrait. The sheer quantity of marinara sauce splattered around her kitchen made it look like a staged *Law & Order* crime scene. Some of it had ended up in her hair—and that of Marcy, who was sitting behind her on the counter, screaming for chicken nuggets.

Judging from Vaughn's comically raised eyebrows when

she yanked the front door open, he'd expected domestic bliss to enfold him like a sugar-spun cloud.

"Hiya…" The hand holding a bunch of daisies dropped to his side. "Doll?"

She was forced to raise her voice over Marcy, who had decided *now* was the perfect time to sing her ABC's at the top of her lungs. "Yeah. *Yeah.* This is what it's like. It's a freaking *free* for all. Okay?" Hearing the crack in her voice, River pinched the bridge of her nose and took a calming breath. "You're thinking of running, aren't you? Like, sprinting down the block at full speed?"

She'd meant it as a joke, but Vaughn's face fell. "No. *Jesus*, no, Riv." His throat worked. "I'm standing here praying you haven't changed your mind. That you'll let me in to…help. Can I help?"

She nodded and took the daisies with a quiet *thank you*, but neither of them moved. "It's not easy, Vaughn. Do you know what you're asking to take on here?"

"Yes," he rasped. "But I'm not asking, I'm begging."

Resisting the urge to massage away the tightness in her throat, River stepped back to allow him inside. It was different from the last time he'd been there. His stepping over the threshold seemed…symbolic. A changing over from before to after. And that observation was so terrifying and real, she shoved it to the back of her mind in an act of self-preservation.

When they walked into the living room, Marcy was throwing herself into a stack of pillows with such dedication, River knew if she forbade the activity, her daughter would only reassert herself with twice the fervor. "Marcy May."

Of course, the child ignored her. River turned to throw a good-natured eye-roll in Vaughn's direction, but froze upon witnessing his reaction to Marcy. At first glance, he appeared… blank. He wasn't moving at all. Maybe not even breathing.

The stillness in the room must have caught Marcy's attention, because she rolled over, a pillow hugged to her chest, and stared back at Vaughn through a messy veil of straw-colored hair. "I want chicken nuggets."

"Where do you…do you have them here? Are they inside or outside?" Vaughn visibly shook himself. "I mean, do we have to go get them or—"

River quieted Vaughn by squeezing his arm. "I have them here." She swallowed a gasp when his hand covered hers, gripping tight. So tight. "Are you okay?" He didn't answer, so she transferred her efforts to her—their—daughter. "Come over here and say hello, Marcy."

"No."

"I brought something," Vaughn said abruptly, before lowering his voice. "I wasn't sure how you felt about gifts or—"

"It's okay." Alarm prickled River at realizing how deep her trust in him still ran. "Whatever you brought is okay."

He appeared dubious, but he reached into his jacket pocket, removing what looked like a photograph. He took a step in Marcy's direction, then stopped short. "Is it…can I?"

Oh God, River was breathing through a cocktail straw. Never in her life had she seen this man so unsure, so out of his depth. And she knew what he needed to come back down to earth. A vision of her and Vaughn intruded—one from a long ago day, after he was released from jail. He'd lain flat on his back, staring at the ceiling while River ran soothing palms up and down his naked chest, whispering nonsense into his ear until he'd come back to her. Looked at her and *seen* her, not the girl who'd sobbed on the sidewalk as he'd pounded another man with his fists.

When River realized she'd been staring into space rather than giving Vaughn his desperately needed answer, she gave a quick nod. "Yes."

He ran scrutinizing eyes over River before advancing further into the living room, hesitating, then crouching down beside a miraculously quiet Marcy. "This is a picture of your mom when she was younger." He set it down on the rug, in Marcy's line of vision, and in true toddler fashion, she snatched the photograph right up, frowning down at it. "You can borrow it for a while, if you want."

His accent was getting thicker, as it always did when his emotions were running high. *When she was younga...you can barra it.* Those dropped consonants never failed to trigger a response deep within her, tug at the connection between them that had apparently never weakened. It relocated her across the room to join Marcy...and Marcy's father...on the floor. "Can I see it?"

Marcy handed over the snapshot—mostly. She insisted on keeping one corner pinched between her tiny fingers. River's laugh broke off when she finally glimpsed the photograph, though. It was taken outside Hook High, the ancient, brick structure looming in the background. River sat on the front bumper of Vaughn's truck, his leather jacket slung around her shoulders, such a contrast to the modest, white eyelet dress she wore. Vaughn was in the picture, too, elbow propped on the truck's hood, looking down at River with a ferocious frown while, in an alarming contrast, she beamed back up at him with unabashed worship.

"I must have been blind," she murmured.

"What was that?"

She brushed off Vaughn's sharp question and handed the picture back to Marcy. "Say thank you for the present."

Marcy side-eyed Vaughn, but a smile teased the ends of her lips. "Thank you."

River retreated to the kitchen to put the daisies in water and stir the spaghetti sauce—where she could still watch the first meeting between father and daughter without participating—because after having her past naïveté presented to her in vivid color, she needed a moment to regroup. Had she imagined the supposed love between her and Vaughn back then? Conjured it up out of sheer force of will?

"Mommy is pretty," Marcy said, still looking at the photograph, poking it with a finger. "She's smiling like that."

River could feel Vaughn watching her, so she ducked into the refrigerator, grabbing the hunk of Parmesan cheese she'd picked up that afternoon. Vaughn's voice drifted into the kitchen. "Does your mom smile a lot, Marcy?"

Heart beginning a dull pound, she closed the refrigerator door to find Marcy holding up the picture, comparing it side by side with River where she stood in the kitchen. Marcy and Vaughn were lying on their stomachs in identical positions, their foreheads wrinkling in the same place, their resemblance apparent for the first time. "She smiles…for me."

Vaughn must have read between the lines of Marcy's answer, same as she had. River put on a happy face for her daughter—the one thing that brought her joy—but smiles for anything personal, save her chats with Jasmine, were few and far between. And based on Vaughn's frown, he didn't like knowing it.

"Mom said you'll stay only a little while."

A flush raked down River's face, moving all the way into her chest when hurt flashed in Vaughn's expression. Hurt followed by stubbornness. She could tell he wanted to contradict what she'd told Marcy, but didn't want to overstep. Especially so soon. And God, she hated having put him in that position, but hadn't it been necessary?

"Tell you what, Marcy." Vaughn's voice was quiet as he addressed his daughter, who watched him with rapt attention. "I *want* to stay longer than a little while. So I'm working on it."

Marcy nodded, then went back to looking at the photograph.

"Dinner in five minutes," River managed.

* * *

Vaughn sat on River's couch, his hands loosely clasped between his knees, staring straight ahead. Because *holy shit*. Dinner with a toddler was no joke. He could hear the low strains of River's voice upstairs as she read Marcy to sleep, and it wrapped around him like a down comforter, fresh from the dryer.

He didn't remember a time when River didn't occupy his heart. His mind. All of him. Her sophomore year at Hook High, she'd passed him in the school parking lot, and magic happened. He'd been a rusted lawnmower forgotten in the shed until River yanked his cord and brought him roaring to life. She'd stopped and stared at him, blonde hair flying around her in the wind, books clutched to her chest—a glowing angel in a gray planet—and he'd lit a cigarette.

God, what an unworthy piece of shit he'd been. Still was. Being in awe of River was a given. She was smart, compassionate, and beautiful. Saw right through him and embraced him anyway. Loved fiercely and took chances. Yeah, he respected River like hell. But watching the way she handled Marcy? He'd only known the half of River's capabilities. He'd sat there like a stool pigeon, frozen in the face of actually doing what he'd set out to do. Be a parent. Help River.

He'd thought winning his family would be the challenge. Turned out, that would only be where it started. Learning to be a…father. That's where he'd need to put in the work.

Vaughn stood and turned upon hearing River descending from above, his breath growing shallow at a sight he never expected to see. River with a finger over her lips, tiptoeing down the stairs so they wouldn't wake *their* child. She still wore the soft pink T-shirt and form-fitting jeans, but might as well have been wearing a dress made of diamonds for how she sent his pulse flying. And God, *goddamn*, he finally understood the saying "You could have knocked me over with a feather." If a flock of seagulls had been passing by, he might have been toast. *Too much good.*

When the finger fell away from her mouth to reveal a frown, when she advanced on him looking worried, Vaughn finally heard the wheezing breaths he was dragging in. It was the same thing that had happened in River's bed the night before, almost like he'd ignored anything resembling feelings for too many years, and now they rushed in to drown him, dragged him to the bottom of the ocean. He'd left her. He'd left his girl crying on the floor, while life swam in her belly, making their child.

"I…uh." Vaughn tugged the hair on the back of his head, until he felt pain. "I'll never be able to do what you do, Riv. Eating with one hand, minding Marcy with the other. Two conversations at once. Having the answer to everything. You…" He stabbed the air with his finger, trying for a casual smile and failing. God, his voice sounded so unnatural. "You're something, doll."

"Hey." River approached him slowly, and he could see the girl breathing side by side with the woman, identical postures forty-nine months and five days apart. How many times had she been required to ease his wild side? "Come here."

A humming noise buzzed in his throat. "I'm making things even harder for you, coming back here. I hate knowing that. But I can't go. I'm sorry."

River finally reached him and the earthquake beneath his feet stilled, those blue eyes firming up the ground. His pulse still sounded like a thunderstorm raging in his ears, but cooling rain had begun, trickling down onto scorched earth. "I know dinner seemed crazy, but it went really well." Her hesitant palms pressed against his stomach. "And I don't want you to go anywhere. This is…good. It's going to be good."

"You don't want me to go?"

"No."

His rough exhale picked up those tiny strands at River's hairline and made them dance. "I just sat there. Didn't know how to help."

Her hands slipped higher, up to his sensitive pectorals and back down. "You'll learn. You'll catch up." A smile teased her lips. "And no parent knows what they're doing all the time, but it's good to know I had you fooled."

Lord, she was being so sweet to him, her palms chafing up and down, that mouth husking words meant to calm. Reading him, knowing exactly what would work to clear the wildfire in his mind, the same way he knew her signals, her needs. River's attempt to ease him might have worked on an emotional level, but certainly not on a physical one. The more she stroked his torso, her bottom lip caught between her teeth, the heavier his groin grew. Without any kind of mental consent, he began pushing his chest into her touch, maybe harder than he should have, because River fell back a step.

But she didn't stop. Thank *God* for that. No, she added the heels of her hands to the mix, raking them down the bumps of his stomach, pressing at his waistband, before dragging them back up to his pecs.

"I should stop." River's breath hitched when Vaughn arched his back, pressing his upper body into the provocative massage. "I'm…it's probably just the memories making me… remembering…"

"The way you used to calm your buck down." Vaughn's tone was like gravel. "Petting me, whispering in my ear about how you love the body that keeps you safe. The body that can't get enough of yours."

Her thumbs met at his belly button, bearing down into the indentation, and Vaughn's cock surged. "Yes," River whispered.

The vulnerability in that single word sliced through the building lust, forcing Vaughn to focus. They were rapidly moving into a stage where he would become single minded in his need for River. But things weren't completely right between them yet. Were they? It was so fucking difficult to tell when she only showed flickers of the pain he'd caused. Over the phone that afternoon, she'd said no to a physical relationship and respecting that wish—respecting River— was something he couldn't take lightly. Not if being part of his own family was his goal.

With incredible reluctance, Vaughn seized River's wrists and ended the torturous massage of his abs. "Have to go. Before we do something that makes you hate me tomorrow."

River gave a jerky nod, but it was impossible not to notice her flushed skin, the way her nipples were peaked beneath the thin, pink cotton shirt. "Okay. You're right."

When she stepped back, Vaughn fought the impulse to yank her close again. His body screamed that River belonged up against him, even as his mind believed the opposite. She didn't belong anywhere near him. Never had. "Night, doll."

Vaughn turned and all but limped to the front door, thanks to the nuclear warhead in his pants, but before he could open it, he heard River move. Heard her feet creak the floorboards. Vaughn didn't face her, but closed his eyes and issued the most heartfelt of prayers that she would ask him to stay. That they wouldn't damn their progress if they obeyed the commands of their bodies.

For the second time that night, Vaughn nearly collapsed, as River's hands snaked around his sides and unsnapped the button of his jeans. "Don't go." She planted a kiss in the middle of his back while slowly lowering his zipper. "I know what I said…and I meant it. This can't be about us. But the *us* won't…"

"Won't be ignored," he managed. "Hell if I don't know all about it, Riv."

A puff of warm air drifted over the back of his neck. "I know it might complicate things, but I need to…"

His control severing, Vaughn pivoted on a heel and grabbed the sides of River's face. "You need what? I'll give it to you. As many times as you can handle."

The blue of her eyes seemed to deepen. "I miss you begging me," she whispered. "I miss being begged for…th-that *one* thing."

"What *one* thing?"

Christ, he was almost shouting. *Take it down a notch.* As soon as he managed to focus on anything but ripping off that pink shirt of hers, he remembered, though. Begging River had never been necessary, except for…

"You want me in your mouth, doll?"

Chapter Eleven

Okay, so maybe River wasn't thinking with her upstairs lady brain. But hell if it hadn't *always* been this way between her and Vaughn. When one of them needed, the other provided. *Loved* providing that balance, fighting one another's insecurities. So when she'd walked down the stairs and seen Vaughn all but vibrating with suppressed emotion? Everything feminine inside her reacted. A red-hot streak of lightning had hit its mark, spreading heat throughout her loins.

Never mind her heart. That traitorous organ had taken a backseat to something else achingly desperate. Maybe *more* so, at the moment. *He's mine to fix. Mine to balance.* A responsibility her body took seriously, if the arousal slickening her flesh was any indication. Vaughn was staring at her mouth like a man obsessed, her lips swelling under that sexual acknowledgment. *I want to be your salvation. I don't care if it's wrong.* She hadn't been lying. Forty-nine months and five days without being the one thing standing between a man—Vaughn—and utter bliss was apparently far too long.

"No," River whispered, sliding her hand down his

corrugated stomach into the opening of his jeans, finding his outrageously full erection and teasing it with light fingertips. "I want you to *put* yourself in my mouth."

He stuffed a hand over his mouth to catch the erupting groan, those hips rocking in rude jerks toward her touch. When the guttural sound died down, he reached out and snagged her jaw. "Let's get one thing straight first." Excitement flashed in River's blood when he got in her face, bringing them nose-to-nose. "You miss me begging you, River? Know this. Each moment I'm awake, *every* part of me begs for—"

Confusion invaded at the cracking of Vaughn's voice, at his visible attempts to gather himself. It didn't make sense. Or maybe it made perfect sense. Maybe the attraction had only ever been physical. In that moment, she could convince herself that suited her just fine. She'd worry about the rest later.

Unwilling to stray from the heat they'd kindled and venture into the dangerous territory of her memories, River ambled backward and slowly removed her T-shirt, pulse stuttering like crazy under Vaughn's perusal. His manhood stood, proud and brutish, in the opening of his jeans, one of his hands hovering an inch away, as if he needed to stroke himself but held back. "Tell me you're sure," he demanded.

She continued her languid retreat, falling onto the couch and pulling her hair back into a ponytail, the way he'd always asked. With that gesture, no other words were necessary. Vaughn wrapped a masculine hand around his length and obliterated the distance to River, straddling her thighs, looming over her in a kneeling position. So familiar, but not. The stakes made it different, but the *lust*… Oh God, the lust, never having faded, had caught them both in an inescapable trap.

"We need that pretty ponytail, don't we, doll?" His fist rode in a tight squeeze up and down his erection, turning it a deeper shade of ruddy tan, right in front of her panting, parted lips. "So I can tear your mouth away when you get too keyed up. You get so excited you forget to breathe sometimes. Isn't that right?"

"Yes," River whimpered, flicking her tongue out to swipe the tip. His *taste*. It was in her blood…and her blood responded to the long lost perfection, pumping, thrilling toward Vaughn. "I need it. Please."

Circling her neck loosely, Vaughn pressed the back of River's head against the cushion, making sure to drape her ponytail over the back of the couch. *For access*, River realized with another aching shiver of longing. "Remember the first time you sucked my dick?" His head fell forward, shook side to side. "You didn't know if you would like it, so we held off. And held off. Until I started dripping in my jeans every time you licked an ice cream cone, or put on that cherry ChapStick. *Fuck*."

There he is. There's that filthy man. Always lurking. Warmth rose up around her like a lazy river, lapping at the notch between her legs. River's hands drifted up her bare stomach to pinch at her nipples, mesmerized by the self-pleasuring hand working overtime. "You always do this." Her voice shook. "You talk until I go crazy."

Vaughn dragged the head of his arousal across River's damp lips. "You love every dirty word. The seam of your jeans is already dark blue." Before River had a chance to respond, Vaughn took advantage of her open mouth, easing his hard flesh inside. "Oh *fuuuuuck*."

River tightened her lips around him and drew back on a long suck, encouraging him with a moan to give her more, but he tugged out of her mouth instead. "*Vaughn—*"

He took River's ponytail and lifted, snapping her spine straight and arching her back. "I asked you a question," he rasped. "Do you remember the first time?"

She took only the smallest pause before she answered. "Yes."

As he wrapped the ponytail around his fist, an answering knot wound itself in River's belly, a delicious, twisting binding that yanked tight when Vaughn spoke again. "You called me in the middle of the night to say you were ready. You know how fast I drove to get to your unfucked mouth?" He dipped the head of his arousal past her eager lips, moved the pulsing flesh back and forth, before slipping back out. "You might have started slow, doll, but by the time it was over, I had to dig your nails out of my ass."

Vaughn's hips rolled forward, pushing his erection to the back of River's throat with a closed-lipped groan.

"Who'd have thought the town sweetheart would have no gag reflex, huh?"

River moaned around the flesh invading her mouth, her hands gliding up the hips that pinned her to the couch. She circled them around to Vaughn's backside, reacquainting her palms with the swell of his taut, rounded male cheeks, stroking her nails downward and enjoying his almost violent shudder. Her ponytail was snared in Vaughn's fist, and he used it as a rein, holding her against the cushion and making sure she didn't follow when he reared his hips back.

"Fuck yeah. Right there, doll. You stay *right there*. Let me sink it in until I can't no more." Accent thickening, he growled through a stilted headshake as he started to pump. "I used to think if someone walked in while I was halfway down your nineteen-year-old throat, they wouldn't believe you'd begged for it. But you did, huh? After that first time, you would pout until I took my cock out and let you play."

River lifted her gaze to Vaughn, barely able to see past eyelids weighed down with lust. Without seeing her own reflection, she knew exactly what he saw there. Something she couldn't hide, even with their confused situation—trust. He'd never pressured her as a young girl into anything. So whether or not he could be trusted with her heart, she gave over her body fully.

And it pushed him over the edge, that unabashed trust. She saw it in the loosening of his jaw, in his thorn-ridden intake of breath. The glide of his hips grew unsteady, even as his erection grew irresistibly swollen in her mouth. "Ah fuck, Riv. Keep looking at me, okay? Please?" He stopped sliding out of her mouth then, simply pressing in tight and rotating his hips, every inch of him beating in her mouth, her throat. His big, muscular body became racked with shudders, saltiness greeting the side of River's throat. "Jesus, *Jesus Christ*," Vaughn gritted out, his grip fierce on her ponytail. "Nothing sweeter. Nothing better than this little mouth. *Missed it*. Missed that tongue, those teeth, that throat. You taste how sore I've been?"

Once Vaughn's shudders of pleasure subsided, they didn't spare a second, both sets of their hands attacking the button and zipper of River's jeans, lowering it with a metallic zing so Vaughn could drop back down to the floor and shove his hand inside. Work-chafed fingers made her panties seem like an annoying formality, yanking them down enough that Vaughn could rub the pad of his thumb on River's clit. Fast, so fast. Aggressive. Sensation slugged her in the center, making relief that had been secondary mere moments before a necessity. Now…now relief was life.

"Faster, more, more…*more*." River spread her thighs wide to give Vaughn room and he took it, sliding her full of those gloriously male fingers. Pumping them into her sex without gentleness. Exactly what she needed. Exactly. "*Yes, Vaughn*."

"You're making me hard again. *Fuck*." He pressed his forehead against River's inner thigh, face screwed up with obvious pain. "No relief. It just never ends, never ends, never…"

He trailed off when River began contracting around his fingers. His head lifted, lust, awe, eagerness battling it out for precedence on his face. River's muscles slung tight, pleasure rushing through, over, around her. Her fingers tunneled into Vaughn's hair, tugging, patting, combing, River having no control of them or idea of their intention. She only knew the atomic bliss that came from having her body satisfied so brutally by a grateful man. Grateful because she'd let him use her mouth. Let him treat it like his personal pleasure device, something that never failed to excite her femininity. Through half-closed eyes, she watched Vaughn fall forward and kiss her stomach, trailing his tongue through the valley of her belly button, traveling sideways to nip at her hipbone.

Finally, Vaughn's head fell into her lap, resting, even as his lethargic fingers attempted to right her panties, his breath still on the shallow side. "What do we do, doll? You told me no messing around. And I'm trying not to screw up this chance." He smoothed his big hand up and down her thigh, warm air from his mouth feathering her bare midriff. "But I don't have the strength to say no when you encourage me. I never did. It's too fucking good when we give in."

River hated the reminder that she was sending mixed signals. One second she pushed Vaughn away, the next it was a race to get his pants off. Truthfully, she didn't know if impulse control was possible with Vaughn. Or maybe…maybe getting physical with him would provide closure. She didn't know. But if he stayed any longer, they would be at it again. No question. And she would be twice as confused when it ended. "I better get to bed. Marcy wakes up early."

• • •

It was the vision of River climbing into bed alone that did it. Another one zoomed in right behind, too. River sleepily preparing breakfast for herself and Marcy in the kitchen. Soft, smiling, sweet. Home. He was supposed to be there. A cutout shape where his body should have been since… always…moved right along River in the shifting images. His life. He wasn't going to keep climbing out the window of his life. Hope—bright and alive—found the dead center of his stomach like a falling meteor.

He'd come to Hook for scraps. Come to collect any small piece of home and family River could give. But he wanted— needed—it all now. *All.* He wanted the love of his life back. Wanted the freedom to sync their hearts again, so bad his blood soared to his head, making him dizzy and determined at the same time. Hell, they were already pounding in time together, it was only a matter of earning the right to acknowledge it, and have *River* acknowledge it, too.

Even though his fighter spirit yearned to pin River down, shove their chests together until she heard the identical beats, common sense had apparently decided to show up. They were adults now, and irrational actions could hurt his chances. He needed to give River time. Time to prove he was the man she'd always needed, but had never gotten. Looking at her now, he could see River's withdrawal, the uncertainty in the way she moved. And while that reaction to their intimacy—intimacy so vital to Vaughn—seared him in agony, it was warranted.

He didn't move right away, but eventually stood, guiding his semi-erect manhood back into his boxer briefs, zipping over the swelling ridge with a barely concealed groan. "I can see you starting to regret letting me touch you, and Jesus, I hate it." He swiped a hand over his mouth. "I want more… *time* with both of you, Riv. More than anything. But I need time with just you, too. To talk. Can you give me that?"

"I don't know," she whispered, a shiver of hope dancing across her features, giving him some in return. "Depends what you want to talk about."

Vaughn shifted in his boots, aching to go forward, to lay everything on the line and accept his sentence. But he staved off the urge, knowing he had a long way to go. So much to prove. "Just think about it."

As he walked out River's front door, he threw one final glance over his shoulder, memorizing the way she looked hugging her elbows, so beautiful, so unsure. *I've got to win her back. I'm done seeing her unsure of me.* Vaughn trudged to his truck beneath the harsh glow of the streetlights, but his heart remained in the house, his identical cut out brushing his teeth alongside River, breathing in the scent of her hair as he fell asleep.

Chapter Twelve

Vaughn's hand shook around the glass of Jack Daniels. It hadn't stopped shaking since Afghanistan. Since the day he'd lost a dozen friends—good men, better soldiers—lost some of his hearing, hell, lost his mind, too, maybe. The sound of a stool scraping back sent Vaughn's heart shooting up into his throat, but he disguised it with a cough and drowned it in whiskey.

Yeah, some of his functioning brain must have shaken loose in the explosion. Why else would he be sitting in the Third Shift while River waited for him at the motel? River. Honest, loving, beautiful, pure white sunlight River. How could he touch her with soiled, shaking hands? How could he look at her without cracking in half? She deserved more than a rotting corpse of a man. Christ, he'd been a shitty choice for River since the beginning, but trying to keep her now—with his head so fucked up—would be a criminal act. He couldn't, could he? Could he?

She would make it all better. He knew she would. Two years she'd waited for him while he completed his tour. That had to mean something, right? Maybe he wasn't a waste of oxygen if

River would wait, even though he'd left in the first place hoping she wouldn't.

Go. Just go to her. She'll heal you.

Vaughn didn't know where the permission had sprung from, but he couldn't move fast enough once it had been issued. He threw money onto the bar, all but diving from his stool—

"Vaughn. Welcome back." River's father appeared to his right, a strange expression on his face, as if he was forcing himself to be polite. But how the older man felt—how he'd always felt—was right there in his eyes. "Where are you headed?"

"You know where." Familiar defensiveness stabbed Vaughn from the inside, but it was dulled now by greater tragedies than merely being disrespected. Life and death tended to put things into perspective, so he forced himself to soften. Even though River's father had clearly loathed him from day one, almost to a confusing degree. Almost as though it went beyond Vaughn dating his daughter. "Look, I thought your daughter might move on if I left. She didn't, though. She didn't. And I can't…I'm not a bastard who can leave her sitting somewhere, wondering where I am." God, just picturing it choked him. "I'm going to do better by her—"

"You can't." River's father picked up a cardboard bar coaster and tapped it against the worn wood. "You've burned all your bridges in this town. There's no way for you to provide for her. You're holding her back by not ending it, dammit."

Vaughn's lungs were on fire, but he had no choice other than to stand there and take the verbal beating. In some sick way, maybe he even wanted to hear it, knowing the sentiments were well deserved.

"I'm not a rich man, either, Vaughn. But I can give her something you can't." He removed a stack of folded papers from his jacket pocket, the top piece stamped with a county seal, just above an address he recognized well. A deed? "When

she finally sees sense and goes to college, the way I never did, she'll have a house to return to, if she chooses. A house. Can you give her that?"

Jesus. No. He couldn't. In this town, you didn't get handed property. It was passed down—if you were lucky—or earned through sweat or blood. He'd lived above an abandoned stationary shop with his uncle, sleeping on a pull-out couch. A safe, warm house was a dream to him—something to aspire to, but unrealistic. Could he take that opportunity away from River?

No. Never. Vaughn fell back into the stool and signaled for another drink, the world having gone dark around him. My life ends here.

Vaughn had only been asleep for an hour when the pounding on his motel room door started. He jackknifed into a sitting position and reached for his weapon, a move that had remained a constant throughout his three different walks of life. Street trash, soldier, security specialist. The coolness of Vaughn's Walther PPS greeted his palm from its position on the bedside table; his feet landed on the tightly woven carpet without a sound. At least his sleepless night hadn't robbed him of his physical abilities along with his mental ones.

Not entirely sleepless. He'd dreamed of the bar. The deed…and the gut-wrenching decision that had come after. If he wanted to earn River's trust back—and he did, more than life—she needed to know what really happened that night. But how did he tell someone he'd lied right to her face, that he'd never stopped loving her—not for a single damn second—but in the course of trying to do the right thing, he'd inadvertently caused life-altering heartache on both of their ends? How did he confess to a lie that had left River a single mother, doing the hardest of jobs alone?

If River hadn't hated him before, she would once she knew. He'd let outside forces keep them apart, when he'd sworn to her countless times he wouldn't. At the very least she would resent him for making such a monumental decision without her consent, or even a conversation.

Vaughn shook his head to clear it of the debilitating memories and approached the motel room door, double-checking the safety was off as he went. Without moving the cheap polyester curtain, Vaughn peeked out through a gap—and found Duke staring back at him from the other side of the window.

With an irritated grunt, Vaughn replaced the safety and unlocked the door. "What the fuck."

"Good morning to you, too, sweetheart," Duke returned, ducking beneath the doorframe to enter the room. "Nice digs."

Vaughn shrugged. "Beats a sleeping bag in the desert."

"Barely," Duke returned, but they exchanged a look, ghosts from overseas floating briefly across their lines of vision. "How's things with River? You two are the talk of the town. Will they rekindle their star-crossed romance or won't they? Everyone is on the edge of their seats."

"Were you always this much of a smart ass?"

"Yes."

The bed groaned beneath Duke's mass as he dropped onto the edge. When he merely crossed his arms and raised an eyebrow, Vaughn cursed under his breath. "Things are…good in some ways, complicated in others. I met Marcy." He felt his mouth bend into a smile and didn't bother trying to dampen it. Not the way he once might have. "She's amazing. I wish I…"

"Spit it out."

He threw his friend a look, wondering why being bullied appeared to be the only way talking came easy. "I wish I had more right to feel proud."

"You'll get there," Duke rumbled.

Vaughn leaned back against the bureau, finally setting his gun down and easing it away. "I told Riv I'm staying, that I want to be a real father. But it doesn't seem right unless I'm River's husband, too. I'm *supposed* to be her husband." He cleared the emotion out of his throat, then threw Duke a look brimming with annoyance. "Why aren't you uncomfortable talking about this?"

Duke's low laugh filled the room. "Man, I've got four sisters at home. They all got married and divorced while we were serving. All of them." He pinched the bridge of his nose. "They always were competitive, but without me here to intercede, it got out of control. Now I've got sisters coming out of my fucking ears. Are you hearing me? My life is non-stop emotion. *Non-stop.* Listening to your shit is a cake walk, compared to what I have to deal with."

By the time Duke finished talking, Vaughn's sides were aching with suppressed laughter. "Sounds like maybe you're the one who needs to talk about his shit."

"I need to be *distracted* from it," Duke clarified. "What do you think I'm doing in this *Miami Vice*-themed junk hole at eight in the damn morning?"

Vaughn held up both hands. "All right, Crawford. I'll distract y—" He broke off when a thought occurred. "Any of those sisters of yours babysit?"

Duke dropped his head into his waiting hands. "Yes. Please give them something to do. Just get them out of the house for *one night* so I can watch *SportsCenter* in my boxers."

"I'll talk to River," Vaughn said. "Actually, that's the whole point. I need to explain what happened before I left." Or *try* anyway. "The talk with her father. What happened overseas. All of it. I just need to get her somewhere we'll actually talk and not—"

"Bang like bunnies on spring break. I hear you." A darker kind of light entered Duke's eyes as he stood. "That's the other reason I'm here. Colonel Moriarty called me again last night. Looking for you."

Discomfort balled in Vaughn's stomach. "What did you tell him?"

Duke's extended silence said it all, but he explained anyway. "I told him you were in Hook for the duration. You *deserve* the damn honor they want to give you, man." He had to speak over Vaughn's grated expletives. "Why do you insist on pretending that night never happened? The army has the right to acknowledge—"

"I don't *want* to be acknowledged," Vaughn shouted. "I don't want some medal and a pat on the back for doing what I signed up for." Pain ticked in his temple, an ache he remembered from that first year back on U.S. soil. "Look—"

Vaughn's cell phone rang on the bedside table, and he bypassed a stone-faced Duke to go answer it. River. Her name came up now, since he'd programmed in her number. Just seeing those five strung-together letters eased his headache. "Hiya, doll," he answered.

"Hey." She sounded distracted, or maybe worried, putting Vaughn on alert. "There's a man at the house here to see you. A Colonel Moriarty? I told him you were staying nearby, so he's having coffee on the back porch...waiting." Silence. "Do you have any idea what he wants?"

"I'll be over in five minutes," Vaughn managed, before hanging up and turning to Duke, anger bubbling in his veins. "You gave him *River's* address?"

"No, I did not." Duke headed for the door. "But if he asked anyone in Hook where to find you, they all would have directed him there, if for no other reason than to fuck with you."

Vaughn snatched up his car keys. "I hate this town."

"No, you don't." Duke preceded him to the parking lot, sauntering toward his own pickup truck, obviously without a care in the world. "I'll send my sisters over later. Good talk."

Chapter Thirteen

River frowned down at the phone in her hand, replaying the brief exchange with Vaughn. Whoever this Colonel Moriarty was, Vaughn didn't seem to be thrilled about having to meet with him. Why?

She leaned into the living room to check on Marcy, finding her wrapped up in a blanket, singing the lyrics from a Disney movie song into a static-ridden karaoke machine. Curiosity eating away at her, River decided not to waste another minute in figuring out what the man on her porch needed. Once Vaughn showed up, she might not get the chance. Even at their closest, secrets had swirled around Vaughn, and somehow River suspected it would be impossible to gain insight if she waited for him to open up. At least about his time with the military. Time she knew nothing about because Vaughn had left Hook the same day he returned.

River slipped out onto the porch, leaving the door ajar so she could hear if Marcy called. Colonel Moriarty watched her through intelligent eyes over the rim of his coffee mug. "Did you get in touch with De Matteo?"

"I did. He's on the way." River cupped her elbows. "Listen, it's probably none of my business, but did Vaughn do something...wrong?"

"Wrong? No." The colonel stood, setting his steaming mug down on the porch railing, the movement very precise. "I've been sitting here wondering why I didn't check for De Matteo at your residence more than once, after my initial search. You were listed as his only next of kin in his file, after all. He would have made his way back eventually."

Pressure shoved against River's sternum, the colonel's words thunking against the inside of her skull. "He listed me as his only next of kin? But he has an uncle..."

When she didn't continue—because there was no one else to list—the man nodded once. "Just you." Whatever he saw on River's face must have interested the colonel, because he tilted his head, squinting eyes that reminded her of old western movies. "Our intention is to bestow the Medal of Honor on Mr. De Matteo, if he would deign to grace us with his presence. I've been seeking Vaughn out since he was discharged."

"Oh my gosh." River sat down out of necessity, pulse going wild in her wrists and neck. A thousand questions occurred at once, so she asked the most insistent. "H-how did he earn the medal?"

He sighed, staring out into the backyard. "We teach them everything but how to communicate to the people back home, don't we?" The colonel considered her for a beat. "I suppose you'll have to hear it from him. But suffice to say, he gave a lot of families closure. Including mine. Which is why tracking him down and ramming the honor down his throat is something of a personal mission to me."

"Oh," was all River managed before Vaughn came bursting onto the porch, hair standing in several different directions, obviously having cut through the side yard. His exhausted gaze seesawed between her and the colonel, before sticking on her, softening. "You didn't tell her, did you, Colonel Moriarty? My River...she shouldn't have to hear terrible things like that."

"No, he didn't tell me. But you will," River whispered, answering for the colonel. Something important was playing out here. She had no idea what. She only knew Vaughn had kept something huge from her, something he'd just confirmed was terrible, and it had happened prior to their breakup. Sensing she wouldn't get a word out of Vaughn until they were alone, she broke their stare and faced the colonel. "How does he receive the honor? Where?"

"I could have brought it with me, but that would be far too easy, De Matteo, after I've spent four years looking for you."

Pain slashed across his features. "I made it pretty difficult to be found."

The older man's eyes briefly floated between Vaughn and River before he took three crisp steps forward. "But find you I did. And we're having a ceremony at Fort Hamilton in two days. It would bring my family great pleasure to have me present you with the medal."

"He'll be there." River blurted the promise, but once it was out, she straightened her spine and owned it. "If you leave me the details, I'll make sure of it."

Vaughn rolled his neck, clearly uncomfortable with so much attention focused on him, but his voice was firm. "Riv, I'm not leaving when I just came back. No way, no how."

She thought back to the young man everyone had discounted except for her. The guy who'd treated her like spun gold, hating himself for bringing her to a motel or his tiny studio apartment. The guy whose parents had abandoned him to TV dinners and an impersonal upbringing via his uncle. And she decided if Vaughn had done something worth honoring, his next of kin should damn well see it carried through. "Marcy and I will come with you. To the ceremony."

His chest lifted and then shuddered down. "You will?"

"Yes," she breathed.

When they managed to break eye contact, the colonel was no longer standing on the porch with them, but they found a note with the time and location of the ceremony inside on the kitchen table. As she scanned the blunt-scripted words, River felt Vaughn's breath coast up her neck. "Come out with me tonight."

Oh Lord, she needed to be with him. Needed the gaps of their history filled in...hell, being around him would be enough. Even now, she felt stronger just having him in the room. More substantial. "I'd have to find a babysitter."

He dragged his bared teeth up River's nape. "Got it covered, doll." They both released a shaky laugh when Marcy screamed for mommy out in the living room. "Be ready at seven."

River nodded, practically deflating when Vaughn released her and backed out onto the porch. Before he could vanish, she murmured, "Are you going to tell me what happened, Vaughn?"

His throat worked. "As much as I can."

He left her wondering exactly what he would leave out. And if, once again, they would be the most important parts.

Chapter Fourteen

Duke dropped off his sisters at seven o'clock sharp and burned rubber down River's street, leaving Vaughn to herd the bickering women into River's house. River had insisted on speaking with Duke on the phone before agreeing to let the sisters watch Marcy, and seemed satisfied with what she'd been told. But it occurred to Vaughn as they arrived at the door that maybe...*he* wouldn't mind being comfortable, too. His time with Marcy so far had been minimal—which he would change as soon as he and River were on even footing—but his daughter's safety had become his concern the moment he'd found out about her.

"Excuse me, ladies," Vaughn said, attempting to cut through an argument about someone's cousin's cousin, who'd apparently married the hairdresser who styled the Real Housewives of New Jersey, but hadn't invited any of them to a filming. Which they all agreed was some righteous bullshit. None of them so much as batted an eyelash at Vaughn's attempt to break into their conversation, so he put two fingers in his mouth and whistled, which in retrospect, might have been a mistake.

"Did you just whistle at us?"

"Do we look like a pack of golden retrievers to you?"

"I knew your uncle, Vaughn De Matteo. He was an asshole, but he sure as shit never whistled at nobody."

"Where's this kid? Are we here to watch a kid or what?"

Vaughn looked down for a moment, before he took a deep breath and tried again. "Look, I'm sorry about the whistling, all right? I'm nervous as hell." He slicked anxious fingers through his hair. "This was my idea. And Marcy's only been my daughter a few days. She's…you know. Perfect. So could you ladies just take good care of her for me?"

There was a long silence—and then Vaughn was smothered by four sets of arms and bosoms, perfume snaking into his throat. Someone was patting his back with such force, he was pretty sure his shoulder blades were being relocated.

"He's cute when he's not demeaning us."

"Not in town three days and he's off the market. This is why. This is why we need to try that online dating."

"I'm going to take that as a yes," he croaked, just in time for the front door to open behind him. River's laugh had the corners of his own mouth lifting. But it was Marcy's shy *hello* that made the network of arms fall away from his body, to the tune of high-pitched squeals. He turned to watch as the four women shuffled Marcy into the living room, pulling toys and coloring books out of various storage spots, turning the space into a full-fledged kid paradise in under a minute. One of the women—whom Duke had introduced as Lisa—removed a makeup bag from her purse and started applying lip balm to a giggling Marcy's mouth.

River stole his attention, though, when she glided into the kitchen to retrieve her purse. Dressed in some kind of wrap-around red dress, she was a stick of fucking dynamite. Christ, he wasn't going to have peace until he'd peeled that clinging material off of her curves and spread her legs. *Please, if you're listening upstairs, let me end the night inside my woman.*

Not an appropriate request for the Big Guy, but then again, he'd never been an appropriate man. Not on his best day.

When River returned from the kitchen, Vaughn wrapped an arm around her waist, losing the ability to breathe when she leaned into his side, resting her head on his shoulder. *This is exactly where I'm supposed to be. Right here.* "Hiya, doll," he murmured. "Marcy will be okay, right?"

River nodded, her forehead nudging his jaw. "She's in heaven." She slipped her hand into his bigger one. "Take me somewhere, Vaughn."

They didn't make it down the porch steps before Vaughn pushed River up against the railing and gave her a slow, wicked kiss. "You trying to stop my heart in that red dress? It might just work." He licked along the underside of her jaw. "You'll have to help me get it ticking again."

She gasped when his teeth snagged on the flesh behind her earlobe. "How am I supposed to do that?"

"Don't make me talk about fucking you. Not out loud. Not yet," he groaned into the crook of her neck. "I'm taking you to eat. We're doing foreplay, you and I."

"Foreplay. Right." River nodded, but yanked him in for a kiss that damn near had steam coming out of his ears, then pulled away with a seductive smile before he could slip her the tongue. Damn. A lot had changed since yesterday, when he couldn't read her. She'd lost that guarded expression, and he was damn grateful. Would it last if he managed to come clean? Vaughn didn't know, but secrets were their enemy at this point. An enemy he'd never be able to defeat without the truth.

As much as he could give.

He beat River to the passenger side of his truck, opening

the door and holding out an assisting hand to boost her up. "Goddamn," he growled when she bent at the waist to duck into the cab, lifting the dress's hem to display smooth, bare thighs. "No panty hose anymore, huh? I can definitely live with that change."

"My mother isn't here to force me into them now." She crossed her legs slowly. "Either way, I don't remember you complaining about them."

"Complaining?" Vaughn rubbed a hand over his open mouth. "I was too busy ripping them off with my teeth."

River's cheeks darkened. "Maybe I should go back inside and put some on."

Vaughn closed the passenger side door, his laugh echoing down the block. Hard as he could, Vaughn tried to hold on to the humor, to retain the lightness River shot into his bloodstream, but as always, the houses caught his attention as they drove. They were in a nicer section of town, residences lit up from within by soft lamplight, gardens blooming in the front yards. *You can't give her that.*

Through sheer force of will, Vaughn shoved aside the plaguing thoughts and focused on now. River sat within his reach. They were actually out together, on a date, and if that wasn't reason to be grateful, nothing was.

He was glad she didn't ask him where they were headed, because her expression when they pulled up in front of Park Place, a small bistro just outside of Hook, was so beautiful, he had to look away. "You remember this place."

"Of course I do," she said after a moment.

"The one time I could afford to buy you a decent meal." He tugged the keys out of the truck's ignition. "Then I ruined the whole night. Your nineteenth *birthday* night. Told you I'd boosted a car in Manhattan to pay for dinner."

Good plan, Vaughn. Start off the night reminding her what a degenerate you were.

"No. You *tried* to ruin the night. I wouldn't let you." River wet her lips. "If I remember correctly, we skipped dessert and went back to your place."

"You're not remembering correctly." He stared out through the front windshield. "I drove us to a park one block over, and you rode me in the backseat."

She uncrossed her legs, but kept them pressed together. "You're not going to make talking easy, saying things like that."

He gave her a look full of meaning. "There won't be nothing easy about what needs saying tonight, doll."

"Okay." Her chest lifted and fell on a deep breath. "Say it anyway."

• • •

Being out with a man, as a woman, while wearing a dress, was a first for River. Because while she treasured the memory of Vaughn taking her out for a birthday dinner at Park Place, she hadn't been a woman anywhere but on paper. This was an entirely new world. A world she'd never entered for two reasons—the daughter she'd loved every moment of raising, despite the hardships, and the man across from her.

Sitting across from any man other than Vaughn would have felt like cheating, even if it were ten years from the day he'd left. Right or wrong, she'd never allowed him to loosen the hold on her. In a way, she'd even reveled in the leftover feelings—the memories, his ultra possessive manner, the euphoria she'd experienced seeing him for the first time. Some people probably went their whole lives without the sensation of flying. What would have been the point in trying to find that again when no one else caused even the mildest reaction?

Her reactions were different now. Tonight. Sitting in

the glow of a crackling fire in her best red dress, she wasn't a bright-eyed teenager anymore. There were stakes in place. No more putting on blinders to Vaughn's issues, pretending everything would be okay. She'd done that once and she'd been blindsided and abandoned for her efforts. River didn't know what would come of Vaughn's return to Hook, but she knew it started with listening. With Vaughn finally talking. With putting aside her own pain and trying to understand.

River ordered a glass of wine, Vaughn a bottle of Budweiser. Both of them were running nervous palms down their thighs, something they noticed at the same time and started to laugh. "Jesus, this feels like a first date," Vaughn muttered. "I guess it is. Guess we're starting from scratch."

"I don't think that's possible for us," River answered, just above a whisper. "The past is too…present."

Vaughn stared at her until the waiter delivered their drinks, then picked up the bottle by its neck and leaned forward. "I know. I know it, Riv. But I wouldn't want to be anywhere else on the goddamn planet right now, okay? Tell me that counts for something."

Her pulse skittered. "It does."

He shoved aside his beer, as if he'd never really wanted it in the first place. "My colonel being there today…this is going to be hard for me to talk about. It's going to be the first time, so I just need to say it."

River barely managed a nod. She wanted to reach out and hold his hand, but he looked too untouchable in that moment, encased in the firelight.

A small silence passed before Vaughn started speaking. "When I was stationed in Afghanistan…" He cleared his throat. "We did these security rounds. Only they lasted hours. Eight of us to a truck, patrolling the zone we'd been assigned." The waiter chose that unfortunate moment to take their order, which they recited quickly and then fell back into a brief silence. "One night—it was at night—we met resistance. Took on enemy fire, which we returned…it seemed to go on forever, Riv. Hours. And I was the only one left standing at the end of it. Out of ammunition, just trying to hide bodies of my guys so they wouldn't get blown apart."

When River lifted a hand to her mouth, Vaughn cursed under his breath.

"I didn't want to tell you this. It makes me crazy knowing you're taking on thoughts like this. From me, especially."

She dropped her hand. "I want to take them on. Please finish telling me."

Beneath the table, Vaughn's foot pressed against River's. "I carried them back. My guys. It took me all night." He wasn't looking at her now. Wasn't seeing her. "I kept thinking the enemy would be back to finish the job, or to clear the road, and they would find me and end it. But they must have moved on to something or someone else, because I got our soldiers back to the perimeter of camp." He pushed the heels of his hands against his eyes. "Just laid them there. But I-I thought it was better than leaving them in the street—"

River broke free from her frozen state, if only to shake her head slowly. Inside, she felt the slow, churning death Vaughn must have experienced that night so far away and wanted to weep for him—for the young man he'd been forced to leave behind—but tears would have to come later, when he'd been reassured. "You did do the right thing," River breathed. "Better than right, Vaughn. All that closure you provided… it was invaluable." She searched around the table, as if the proper words would appear on the floor. "I'm so proud of you."

A sound left him, a gruff heave of weight leaving his chest. The muscles in his throat moved up and down. "Proud of *me*? Look what you've done with our child. She's incredible thanks to you, Riv. I'm proud of *you*." The intensity in his gaze hit her like a ton of bricks. "You know what, though? If you have pride in me, I'm not going to question it. I don't care about anything else in this life. Nothing but that. Is that wrong?"

Confusion banded together with the tumult of emotions she was experiencing. Had she been a support system for him so long he'd stopped loving her somewhere along the way, becoming dependent instead?

"There." He pointed at River from across the table, dark brows drawn close. "Where did you just go on me?"

Selfish. Stop being so selfish. He'd just told her something traumatic, something more important than a young girl's heartbreak, and she was thinking of herself. River forced steel into her spine. "Nowhere. I'm right here." Taking a chance, she reached across the table and twined their fingers together. "Right here."

Vaughn's skepticism still showed on his handsome face, even as he leaned in, his voice turning gruff. "I'd love us to be somewhere I could make sure of that."

River's heartbeat tripled, the restaurant's temperature seeming to increase to an inferno state. *Comfort him*, a voice urged in the back of her mind. Was Vaughn distracting her from an important conversation with sex? Yes. He always did. Would she give in anyway, if that were the case? Relaying the story had obviously taken its toll on Vaughn, leaving his eyes haunted, his mouth set in a grim line. However that long ago night had turned out, he'd needed her, whether he'd loved her or not. And he needed her again tonight, with the wound having reopened. "Let's get the food to go."

His hand clenched into a fist inside hers. "Go where?"

Her thighs tightened just thinking about it. All those stolen, forbidden hours, being taken roughly on a cheap comforter, traffic whirring past outside. Closure. That's what the motel represented. If Vaughn didn't love her, maybe she could at least get closure. A way to move on with Vaughn in her life, without the bone-deep longing that came along with being near him. "You know where."

Horror registered, darkening his expression. "I'm not taking you back there."

River could see he meant it, that he wouldn't change his mind unless she convinced him. Beneath the table, she placed her hand on Vaughn's knee and slid it up, up until she reached mid-thigh. "Let's replace a bad memory with a good one." She pressed her thumb into the meat of his inner thigh, circling it in a sensual massage, making Vaughn close his eyes on a low groan. "Take me to our place."

Chapter Fifteen

"Don't go. Don't go."

River lunged from where she lay in a sobbing heap on the bed, latching onto Vaughn's arm before he could reach the door. Leaving? Just…leaving? This couldn't possibly be real. Yes, it was a horrible nightmare. He hadn't meant anything he'd said. How could he have stopped loving her when she had enough love inside her for them both?

"Let me go, River." Dull eyes stared clear over her head. "I said what I came to say. Should have said it a long time ago."

"No, you're lying." *She screamed at him, smacking her palms against his immovable chest. "I can prove it."*

A spark of the old Vaughn made her breath catch. Maybe it was her feverish denial, projecting what she needed to see to survive, but she swore he'd glanced down at her with a flash of unsuppressed hunger. Without time to reevaluate, River tore the dress over her head, leaving herself standing before Vaughn in nothing but the special, lacy white thong she'd bought in anticipation of his return. The air conditioning teamed up with Vaughn's blistering stare to pebble her nipples into aching little points.

And then it was Vaughn's turn to lunge. With a ragged sound he tackled River onto the bed, shredding her panties in desperate hands. "Fuck, doll. Why are you doing this to me? I left my condoms in the car," he growled. "I knew I'd want this."

She could feel Vaughn reining himself in, knew by his deep drags of breath, he was attempting to gain control and stop. Stop touching her. No. God, no. If she let him walk out the door, she wouldn't have another chance to get through to him. This—touching—was how they'd always broken down barriers. If he left now, she would never see him again. The panic rose in her throat until near hysteria trickled in, bleeding past the edges of her mind.

I'm losing him. I'm losing him.

"I'm on the pill," she said on a shudder, grasping at the only lifeline available to her. Because surely if he left, she wouldn't be able to open her eyes and see the next morning. "I went on it for us."

Misery laced Vaughn's blissed out groan when he plunged into her body, pumping into her with jarring force, driving River's slight body up the bed.

With the love of her life's breath shallow and rasping in her ear, River let her eyes fall shut, arms tightening around him in a fierce hug. "See? You love me." Her voice shook with the reverberations of Vaughn's frantic thrusts. "You love me. I know you do."

He proved her wrong half an hour later when he stumbled out of the room without a backward glance.

Vaughn couldn't believe he'd let River convince him to go back to the motel. Sure, he was staying there for the time being. But River standing in the parking lot beside him was like a heart-wrenching flashback. One that was happening in real time. Making matters worse, her hand was tucked trustingly inside his. The bastard who'd ripped their future—and her delicate heart—in half the last time they'd been there together.

When they walked into his room, he watched her take a turn around the bed, the chair he'd been using as a clotheshorse. Nothing had changed since they'd stayed there. Same color scheme, furniture, and background noise. Everything had remained the same, apart from him and River. A memory of her balled up on the bed, tears staining her cheeks, moved across his consciousness, and he had to look away, setting the to-go containers on the round, wobbly table opposite the bed.

"Maybe we should have taken the booze with us, too," Vaughn muttered, chancing a glance at River.

She raised an eyebrow, and with a little flourish, she pulled the corked bottle of wine out of her purse. "Would have been a shame to let it go to waste."

Love pummeled him with such force, honesty escaped as though an emergency valve had been turned. When he spoke, his words were labored. "I lied."

Her smile slipped, the bottle of wine dropping to her side. "Sorry?"

God, he thought the words would feel like rose bushes being ripped out through his throat, but having made the initial admission, the rest flowed out like water that had been dammed too long—until he saw the dawning recognition on River's face, saw her lower herself to the bed in slow motion. "I lied that night, Riv," he said hoarsely. "You think I could've stopped loving you so easily?"

She didn't answer. Didn't move.

"I was dying for you," he near-shouted, falling into the single dining chair. "Don't you see, though? That was the problem. It was *always* the problem. The day we met, I started sucking all the possibilities out of you. College. A job and a life outside of this town." She was facing away from him now. There. He'd lost her for good, hadn't he? The lie that kept on giving. "You couldn't just move on while I was away. Or hell, see sense while I was still fucking *here*. You just kept running to me, and I couldn't let myself catch you again. I had no choice that night, River. Before I left, I was bad for you. When I came back..." Vaughn shook his head. "I was flying shrapnel. I knew even less how to be the man you deserved."

He closed his eyes and remembered the night in the Third Shift when River's father had forced him to see sense. Forced him to admit he was killing River in his own inexcusable way. River didn't need to know what had pushed him into the lie, though. It would only hurt her more—possibly dent her relationship with her father—and he was done causing her pain.

"So you..." River started quietly, face still turned away. "You did love me."

Humorless laughter rattled in his chest. "You couldn't feel it? I damn near smothered you on that bed. Jesus, I couldn't let your mouth go long enough to give you a decent breath." Vaughn shoved to his feet and paced to the door. "Walking out of here was like having my goddamn limbs torn off."

When he turned around, River was standing, too, watching him across the room through luminous blue eyes. *I still love you*, Vaughn wanted to shout. *I'd murder, sacrifice, and starve for you.* But it would be too soon when he'd just ripped open the old wound.

"So you made that decision for both of us?" River murmured, rounding the bed and coming toward him. God, if she tried to get past him to the door, Vaughn couldn't promise he wouldn't block her, get on his knees, and beg her to stay. She didn't attempt to exit, however, stopping instead when they were toe-to-toe. "You just decided I wouldn't try to compromise or make our relationship all right for both of us?

I'd grown up while you were gone. And we loved each other enough to make it work."

Not enough to give you a real home. A safe, secure one. With a deed attached.

"There was no compromise. I couldn't support you then—I didn't know how." He raked stiff fingers through his hair. "I made the decision I thought was best for you. You were the only thing that *ever* mattered."

River opened her mouth then closed it, falling back a step in a way that made Vaughn frown. "God, I-I really want to hate you for making that decision for us, but I…"

He stepped forward, countering River's backward progress. "You what, doll?"

"I made a decision for us, too. That night. Or maybe it wasn't a decision at all, because I barely remember anything past being so scared. I didn't know how to reach you." Her voice hitched on the last word, one hand coming to rest on her throat. "Maybe I hadn't grown up while you were gone. Not as much as I thought. I was a grown woman, and I didn't even consider the consequences…of sleeping together without…" She blew a breath up at the ceiling. "I wasn't on the pill."

Gravity pushed down on Vaughn's shoulders, even as his insides seemed to elevate, straight up into his neck. "You…" He cleared the rust from his voice. "You weren't on the pill."

River spoke in a whisper. "No." She fell back a few more steps toward the bed, and Vaughn stalked her, lifting his hands to clamp them on either side of her face. "It was wrong. Lying about something so damn important. I *know* it. But I never would have tried to trap you. It's why I didn't try to find you…I refused to even let myself look. It's why I've given you as many outs as I could since you came back."

Vaughn erupted forward, branding River's mouth in a kiss that lacked all control. In an achingly familiar move, they fell back on the bed, River arching beneath him, wrapping her legs around his waist with a whimper. His hands couldn't get satisfaction, roaming down her thighs, squeezing her knees, racing up into her hair. She slapped at his shoulders, writhing beneath him to signal she needed to breathe, and he barely managed to release her mouth. "Our first time without a condom." His words emerged like shards of glass tearing through muslin. "Christ, I can still remember your hands on my ass, yanking me closer when I came, legs open so wide for it. Oh God, Riv—"

"I should be more sorry," she breathed. "I know I should, but I can't be."

She was so damn beautiful, blonde hair fanned out behind her on the bed, it took Vaughn a moment to speak through the crowding of emotion. "I'm not sorry, either, River. You hear me?" He swallowed the growing lump in his throat. "I'll thank God every day for the rest of my life you did what you did. It's why we're here together now."

• • •

For long moments, they simply breathed into each other's mouths, blue eyes searching brown, but those exhales turned to pants in short order. River's relief had freed her, blowing exhilaration up her spine. *He'd loved her.* Vaughn had loved her, and he didn't condemn her now for the reckless attempt to reach him she'd made in the heat of the moment, trying to connect with him some how, some way.

Laying on that crappy motel bed, they were survivors of a self-imposed disaster, and healing became River's sole purpose, her hands raking down Vaughn's back to grasp the tight curve of his buttocks, encouraging him to rock against her, to use her as shelter from the fallout from the truth bomb they'd just set off.

"Take me hard," River husked, licking the rough skin of

Vaughn's neck as it vibrated with a starved growl. "Make me scream. Make me feel you in my stomach."

Her last word ended on a moan when Vaughn pulled her wrists up, crossing them above her head, driving into the notch of her thighs at the same time. "You think after forty-nine months and six days without my woman's pussy, I'm going to make love to her like some soppy fucking poet, Riv?" He craned his neck to hiss against the valley between her breasts. "Spread your thighs. The way you did that night for my bare cock."

Wicked flashes of pleasure went off at the tips of her nerve endings, a reaction her body knew would only ever come from Vaughn. But something he'd said paused the progress of her knees falling open. "Forty-nine months and six days…"

She gasped when Vaughn caught her jaw, his fingers firm and unyielding. "No one else. You hear me? There's been *no one else*." Using both of his knees, he widened her thighs with a merciless push. "I've spent this whole time behaving as if we were married. It's the only way I could stay sane. Making believe you were my wife and I'd see you when I got home at night. Maybe I'm a crazy man. I don't know. I don't—"

River freed one of her hands locked above her head, slapping it over Vaughn's mouth. Her heart had reached its fill line and brimmed over. It couldn't handle another jolt from the invisible electric paddles in Vaughn's hands. Between them, their harsh breaths whirled, chests heaving as they stared across the scant inch separating their mouths. "You're *my* crazy man." She tilted her hips beneath him, sliding them back and forth against his huge, protruding erection. "Remind me how crazy, Vaughn."

His eyes flickered from aroused to grave for a split second. "Be careful what you wish for, doll." Throat working up and down, Vaughn reached behind his head, snagged his shirt and yanked it off, baring the rough-hewn body of her fantasies.

But, *oh God*, it was different. *Different* didn't do it justice.

River reached out with gentle fingers and traced the jagged, violent, inked-over scars marring his once-perfect chest. Scars carved in the shape of her name, so crude they appeared as if they'd been inflicted with a dagger. A sound tripped over her trembling lips. "What did you do?"

"I needed something to remind me I'd been lucky once," Vaughn murmured. "I know it's not pretty, Riv, but that ain't nothing compared to waking up and trying to…exist without you."

His admission cut the leash on something wild inside of her. Frantic for a more substantial connection with the man staring down at her like he could suck in his final breath at any moment, River wedged her hands between them, unbuttoning Vaughn's jeans. Heavy lids came down to conceal his eyes, that stubbled jaw going slack. "Do you have a—"

"In my pocket." Vaughn's eyes blazed open. "Wrap it up this time, you understand? I need about ten years of fucking you without a break. Just want to slide right up inside my woman's pussy and remind the back of it what my tip feels like." He slipped a hand between River's thighs, twisting his hand in her panties and tearing them off. "*Mmmm*. You kept it warm for me."

"*Yes*." Lord, she'd missed the way he spoke to her. The way no one had ever dared, as if they were two objects put on this earth for the sole purpose of providing pleasure, giving them permission to touch, talk, move how they wanted. With frantic fingers, she delved into his pocket to locate the condom, holding it between her teeth as she unzipped his pants, whimpering and sobbing the whole time.

The muscles in Vaughn's arms, neck, and chest flexed, his eyes squeezed closed, his mouth chanting the word *hurry*, again and again. River thought he would drive himself inside her the moment she'd seen to their protection—she *needed* him to—

but he took her by surprise, sliding off the bed's edge and positioning his mouth just above her damp femininity, hovering there as he perused her beneath half-closed lids.

River lifted her hips with a needy sound. "Please."

"*Stop that begging*," he growled. "I'm doing this right, begging for *you* this time around." His stiffened tongue dragged through her folds. "Asking you to please let me ram my cock into this pretty flesh. Need it. Need you. Need you so bad."

Already, the high, inner section of her thighs was beginning to spasm, but Vaughn must have felt the tremors, because he pinned her limbs onto the bed. "Y-yes," she cried out through clenched teeth. "*Yes*, you can have me."

She clapped a hand over her mouth to stop from screaming when Vaughn's tongue began to flick against her clit *relentlessly*, making it swell above the deep, resonating buzz of lust. "Love everything about this pussy. My too-tight second home," he said, laying a hot, tongue kiss over her sensitive nub, before rising above River and planting a hand on the mattress. A gruff breath heaved past Vaughn's lips as he thrust into her, his foul curse coloring the air. "And you... you're my first home, Riv. Always have been," he said shakily. "But I'm about to demolish you."

Reunion. Her mind and body synched for the first time in years. She gasped for air and felt her lungs fill to a capacity she'd forgotten them capable of. The evidence of their irrevocable attraction pulsed between her legs, stretching flesh that remembered him, craved him. Thrills raced up her middle, starting at the point he ended and River began, although that line blurred and vanished when Vaughn dragged her hips to the bed's edge. She expected their first time in four years to be fast and hard, but Vaughn's heated expression told her he had other plans.

When Vaughn knelt on the floor, he took River with him, holding her against the mattress drop-off until only the tip of his huge erection remained inside her. And then he let go, allowing River to slip down and impale herself with a close-mouthed scream.

Vaughn's head fell back, sensual mouth opening on a long, vile *fuuuuck*. "I could have done so much more with all those hours together, Riv. I think about how I missed out on taking you in so many different positions. God, all the ways I could have banged you if I'd just had some patience." His hips ground in an up and back pattern beneath her, creating a sweet sizzle in her clit as his body massaged her at the deepest possible point. "It was all about getting inside you, wearing you out, slapping my balls up against that schoolgirl ass. I still want to, don't I? I'd like to flip you over and get my nut, but I'm a man now. And you're going to be treated like a woman on my watch. Say my name if you understand me."

"Vaughn," she breathed, widening her thighs and attempting to ride him, but big hands on her backside kept her seated and still. "Vaughn. *Vaughn.*"

"That's the only name you'll ever say on the way to an orgasm."

River's nod was frantic, her teeth beginning to chatter, courtesy of the desire grabbing hold of her nervous system, of every part of her. With that silent agreement, Vaughn surged up, positioning her bottom just beneath the edge of the mattress, hooking his arms beneath her knees. Then he began to drill into her slowly. A nasty, yet unhurried entering of her body. A torturous slide out. The mind-blowing journey back to her stopping point. The hot press of his balls against the crease of her backside. "Oh…faster, please," River sobbed. "Too long. It's been too long."

"What did I say about that begging? It's *my* goddamn turn," Vaughn reminded her hoarsely, craning his neck to suck a pebbled nipple between his lips. And when he spoke again, his gaze was fastened between her spread legs. "Can I have this pussy for myself again? Please, River? Give it back to your buck for safe keeping."

A shudder drove through her like a hundred mile an hour wind. The word *yes* bounced up and down on her tongue, but it wouldn't come out. Some shred of self-preservation begged her not to make *the* almighty decision when her body was on fire. And it was. She was engulfed by a blaze that had never really gone out, but had been renewed even hotter than before.

It was clear from the inferno reflecting back in Vaughn's eyes that he didn't appreciate her hesitation. The pace of his thrusts grew more biting, more insistent, his flesh entering her with hard slaps. "My baby doll needs more persuading, does she?" He added a twist of his hips to the sensuous pattern in which he drove into River's body. There was a stiff set to his jaw, but those brown eyes were pleading and desperate, calling to the organ in her chest. "Please, oh God, *please.* I can't live on memories anymore." He fell forward, planting his sweat-dappled face against her neck. "I've hated my cock. I've abused it, because it wasn't making you come. I've been so rough with it, holding off until a single thought of you could make me bust in my pants. It's been my enemy." His rush of breath slithered through her hair. "Because it wasn't here where it was supposed to be, satisfying these dirty little needs I created in you. I did, didn't I? Made a good girl dirty?"

"*Yes,*" she wailed up at the ceiling. During Vaughn's speech, the pumps of his hips had lost their rhythm, but River's pulse still accommodated the erratic beats, matching it, made for it. "You made me dirty."

His answering growl was accompanied by the last vestige of his control slipping. River felt the snap, felt the impact of restraint being lost. He began thrusting into her so hard the upper half of her body bowed back, hands fisting in her own hair. She could feel the rebounding of her breasts with every pounding of Vaughn's body, and that sexual hyperawareness was heaven, earth, and everything in between. Especially when Vaughn's teeth raked down the center of her body, from her cleavage, downward.

"Oh. Oh *God*," River gasped, feeling her loins tighten and quiver. "*Yes*."

When Vaughn forced them both fully up onto the bed, the gravitational press of his body robbed River of lucid thought. As if every component of their beings craved contact, their left hands met and held above River's head. "This is where I'd turn you over and fuck anything I want to hear out of your mouth, isn't it?" His right hand slid between their married hips, the pad of his thumb giving her clit the attention it craved. "This kitty likes when you're on all fours, doesn't it? You could never get that ass up in the air fast enough. *Fuck*, the way you used to look at me over your shoulder. Come get it, big daddy." He broke off on a growl, releasing the hand he'd pinned above her head in order to grip her leg. "*Next time*. This time I'm begging to get back between these thighs. Permanently. I want it every goddamn day."

River's right knee was jerked up to her shoulder, Vaughn coming at her from an angle that ripped a scream from her mouth. Every pound of his formidable body drove her across the bed, her hands alternating between slapping him across the face and yanking his hair, urging him closer. Here was familiar. This place where her lover—Vaughn, *always* Vaughn—stole her humanity. Turned her into a climax-hungry animal, clawing, reaching, twisting.

And then the orgasm pummeled River, locking her muscles into a shaking tangle with Vaughn's. She could hear his voice in the distance—and he was angry, in a breathless, awed sort of way.

"No. *No.* I needed you to take me back first," Vaughn shouted into her shoulder, seconds before he lifted his head, giving River a front row seat to his eyes going blank, his jaw slackening. His masculine rumble of completion pushed her higher, prolonging the climax, doubling its potency. "Finally coming in what's mine again. Finally. *Finally.* Say the words, doll. Please."

She found the strength to move her head, pushing her lips up against his ear. "My body will always be yours, Vaughn. Always."

With a broken sound, Vaughn moved down River's body, slipping his sweaty forehead between her breasts. "Need this heart back, too. This beautiful heart." He turned his ear to her chest, listening for a moment to the rapid beat before nodding, pressing his lips to the fluttering flesh directly above the clenching organ. "I'm sorry to you most of all."

Chapter Sixteen

Vaughn could barely keep his eyes on the road as he drove River home. God, with the amount of time he'd spent inside her body in his lifetime, one would think he'd have had an accurate memory of the sensation. The clenching, the sliding, the push and pull. In his mind, his groin, his stomach. Everywhere. They were fucking magic in bed together. There was no way around it. Before setting eyes on River that day in the school parking lot, he'd been with other girls. Not hundreds, but enough that he needed two hands to count. And yet something deep in the pit of his soul had compelled him to wait for River once they'd met eyes, swearing off all others. Thank God for that elusive something. Thank *God*.

A similar prayer had gone into tattooing her name across his chest. He'd been working a security job, escorting the family of a visiting businessman to and from their various activities while the guy worked. One afternoon, while waiting for the wife to emerge from a lunch meeting, he'd been standing on the sidewalk outside the restaurant, and swore he'd seen River walk by. He'd run. Without a thought, he'd been in a dead sprint toward the feather-light blonde hair floating on the wind. His lungs were burning, eyes gritty by the time he stopped, realizing he must have imagined her.

That night, he'd gone home and, using a prison yard technique, added her name to his flesh, ink and blood drying into the carved up skin. Maybe enjoying the pain meant he was sick, but he'd needed to divert the ache coming from deeper inside. And with the pain of being without River growing worse with each passing day, he'd known getting over her was a pipe dream. So he'd resigned himself to living with the agony and *needed* a representation of it. Something tangible.

Showing River tonight what he'd done had been the ultimate high, although he couldn't account for why. He only knew watching her eyes run over the letters, hearing her breath catch, had healed something he'd thought never would be soothed, a raging that had been living under his bones for so long.

Unfortunately, she yet hadn't vocalized whether she would allow the soothing balm she provided to spread over every part of him. She hadn't put him out of his misery and taken him back. While he appreciated her need to be cautious and process everything through the eyes of adulthood, it was killing him. The silence, the fact that no part of them was touching…everything about waiting hurt.

Vaughn pulled his truck to a stop outside River's house and cut the engine, neither of them making a move to alight. "Something tells me my house is a wreck."

His mouth edged up. "Hire a cleaning service, and we'll send Duke the bill."

"Or we could just put him in a maid outfit and have him clean it himself."

"Now there's an idea," Vaughn laughed. When the sound faded, he knew the elephant in the truck had to be addressed.

"Look, Riv—"

"Yes," she blurted.

His pulse skittered, hands clutching the steering wheel so hard they shook. "Yes to what?"

She turned shimmering blue eyes on him. "Maybe I'm crazy, but I want to try…us again. I'm thinking maybe it would be crazier if we didn't." Her laugh was watery and self-conscious. "Okay?"

"Okay?" He could barely speak around the relief pressing against the walls of his throat. "Yeah, Riv, that's pretty fuckin' okay."

"Okay," she breathed, blonde hair falling across her face when she ducked her head, probably to hide the flush creeping up her smooth cheeks. But when their gazes met again, he saw there was more, could feel purpose radiating from her. "Tonight at dinner…the way you talked to me. I need that all the time, Vaughn. No more keeping things to yourself. We can't be a team otherwise." She paused. "Please?"

"Yes." The word ripped out of him, because what else could he do or say when *life* was bleeding back into his body? River. He was getting a second chance with River. *"Yes."* They stared at one another across the console a moment, before she turned to exit the truck. But she paused. And then she was launching herself across the truck's cab at Vaughn, who'd been halfway to diving after her if she'd actually managed to escape. "Where were you going, huh?" He growled against her mouth. "You were just going to sneak out after that, doll?"

"It's silly. I *know* it's silly. You just…*we* just…"

"Fucked like the world was ending." He smoothed a hand down her ass, ran a finger up through the sweet divide in the center. "Invite me in, and we'll end it for good. Burn the motherfucker right on down."

"I can't yet." She kissed the underside of his jaw, then slid back to his ear, delivering a groin-tightening lick. "We have to ease into this. Marcy can't wake up one day and find you sleeping in my bed."

Vaughn nodded through the ache in his gut, knowing she had a point. "Okay, doll. You're right. I just…Christ, I want to hold you while you sleep again. I never stopped taking that job seriously."

"Soon." Their mouths locked together, tongues competing for the best taste, before River pulled back. "Soon…I hope. Taking this slow isn't just because of Marcy. I've spent a lot of time thinking you didn't want me. Just let me get used to you again."

Ah God. She didn't mean to twist the wrench in his chest, it was just a casualty of the war they'd been fighting to stay alive while apart. Vaughn wrapped two fistfuls of blonde hair in his hands and tugged her close, pressing their foreheads together. "As long as it takes, Riv. I'm staying right here."

Forever starved for River's mouth, Vaughn moved in again, but River evaded him. "Vaughn." That pink tongue skated across the seam of her lips. "What happened that night overseas, and the hard time you had coping…is that the only reason you left? Because you didn't want to burden me with it?"

An image of the deed flickered in his conscious, but the truth never made it out. He was too close to having her back. And God knew, he would not only fuck up the explanation, but the relationship between River and her father, a relationship he'd never had with his own. "I couldn't ask you to heal more of me, doll," he finally pushed through stiff lips. "You'd already wasted enough time doing that."

"It's not a waste," she whispered. "It never was."

They shared one final desperate kiss, pulling away with a mutual groan. Watching River climb the stairs to her house, the past collided with the present, creating a sense of completion so strong, he couldn't house it all, even as the necessary lie by omission tried to roam his mental hallways.

Hope grew, sprouting green and rolling into fields... until Vaughn went to put the truck in gear and saw River's father parked in a running car across the street. The older man glanced toward the house, then back at Vaughn, before pulling away from the curb and disappearing down the block.

• • •

From the corner of her eye, River observed Vaughn squashed into the driver's seat of her red Pontiac—his white-knuckle grip on the steering wheel, the stress around his mouth. Before they'd loaded into the car in preparation for the drive to the ceremony at Fort Hamilton he'd been jumpy, but refused to say why. When she'd noticed him go still as she strapped Marcy into her car seat, she'd realized it was his first time driving with a toddler in the backseat.

"Jesus, I was less nervous driving a Humvee," he admitted now, raking blunt-fingered hands through his hair. "Did you... how do you decide which car seat to buy? Don't any of them come with a steel cage around them?"

River laughed into the paper cup of coffee he'd brought her from the deli. "The first time I took her to the supermarket, I kept checking the rearview mirror, double checking I didn't accidentally leave her on the sidewalk or something."

He cast her a measuring look. "How did you hold her and shop at the same time?"

She rolled her shoulders forward. "They have these slings—"

"You used one of those?" The muscles in his throat moved in a pattern as he swallowed. "Do you have any pictures of you wearing it?"

"Somewhere," she murmured. "Probably."

"I'd like to see that." His brows drew together. "One of

you in the hospital. One of you feeding her. Even the bad, out of focus pictures. I want to see them all."

River had to stare out the side window a moment. "They're in the attic, most of the earlier ones. I'll dig them out."

"I can do it." His glance in her direction was rife with meaning. "I'll be around."

His focus returned to the road, but she could almost sense the scattering of his thoughts, could see him shift from determined to pensive and back again. Would this man always be a little bit of a mystery to her? Would his mind's inner workings, when finally confessed, always surprise her somewhat? *Not* looking at him and wondering was worse— she knew that from experience—but the yearning for total honesty wouldn't be swept aside, either.

Noticing Marcy had dozed off in her car seat, River leaned her head against the passenger side window and closed her eyes. Last night had been...odd. Her father had shown up on her doorstep out of the blue, holding a present for Marcy. A fishing trip to upstate New York with his old buddies had been his explanation for showing up in Hook. But showing up without warning and without her mother in tow? It was strange, to say the least. And she'd gotten the distinct impression the full picture wasn't clear yet.

When she'd explained where they were going the following morning—with Vaughn—he hadn't bothered to disguise his displeasure, his silence on the matter speaking volumes. Without a word, he'd taken River's set of spare house keys and gone to bed down in the guest room, saying only that he would see her when she got home. Growing up, her family had learned to do things on her father's time. He rarely explained himself or worried about inconveniencing others. But his sudden arrival at her house seemed to go further than inconsiderate behavior.

River could still recall how uneasy Vaughn had been on those rare occasions when he and her father were in the same place at the same time, while he waited on the porch for her, or they passed her father in town. It was almost like an invisible hostility settled over everything. The timing of his arrival made her nervous, much as she told herself to stop worrying. She and Vaughn were adults now. They made their own decisions, and nothing could affect the new start they were allowing themselves.

Vowing to worry about her father when she got home, River focused on Marcy and Vaughn. The honor he would receive that night. How much it meant to him.

They arrived at the hotel arranged for them through the army administration—far fancier than she'd expected— and found a loaned dress uniform waiting for Vaughn at the front desk, which he'd taken with a smirk. They'd boarded the elevator with Marcy on Vaughn's shoulders, making it necessary for her to duck down, little arms wrapped around his face. The combination of masculine laughter and little girl giggling floated through River's mind now as she took her seat with Marcy, in the third row of the ceremony hall.

"Mommy, where's Vaughn?"

"I don't know," River said softly, smoothing her touch down the back of Marcy's hair. There had been a last minute rehearsal when Vaughn agreed to attend the honoring ceremony, so he'd been forced to jet, garment bag thrown over his shoulder, as soon as they reached the hotel. But she hadn't missed his reaction to the suite…the second room with the separating door. Or the promise in his eyes as the hotel room door closed behind him.

The answering flutters in River's stomach still hadn't subsided…but when Vaughn walked out onto the stage and took a seat, breathing became a laughable aspiration. *No way.* No way that was the same guy who wore ripped jeans and threadbare T-shirts even in the dead of winter. There was no way to describe him, apart from…heroic. Gorgeous. Male. Slightly agitated by the crowd's presence, sure, but that only endeared him more to River. Because she could see the taciturn young Vaughn underneath the uniform, and she could see the man he didn't even yet realize he'd become. And they were both incredible.

Vaughn's gaze ran over the crowd, hand tugging on the stiff collar of his shirt, the restless movements stilling when their eyes locked. "There's your daddy," River whispered to Marcy, without thinking. She didn't have to think. The words just rolled out, sounding perfect and right and maybe even overdue to her ears.

Marcy tilted her head, bumping cheeks with River. "Daddy." She whispered the word, smiling wider than River had ever seen. "He's going to stay a long time?"

River sucked in a breath and let it out slowly. "Yes. He's staying."

Chapter Seventeen

Until he'd met River, there had been very few moments Vaughn wanted to remember—to freeze in time and carry around, thawing them out when he needed a fix of something good. Since the moments from his first eighteen years were shitty, he'd been determined to make even worse ones. Block out the pain of being left behind by his parents, by garnering new clips of memorized time. Ones he could control. Getting into fights, stealing cars, drinking. If good moments wouldn't be forthcoming, he would prove he didn't need them.

And then he'd seen River in the parking lot outside Hook High, and the memory had frozen itself, without his consent, crystalized in all its perfection, never to be chipped or fogged. Another one had immortalized itself when she'd set her books down on the back bumper of his truck, wet her lips nervously, and kissed him…on the cheek. The way she'd pulled back with brave eyes and hard nipples. Two very different sides of a shiny, new coin he didn't deserve to have in his pocket, but one that wouldn't stop turning up, making him wish, making him hope.

Before tonight, he'd seen pride in River's eyes, but it had always been unfounded. Undeserved. Had something changed? Yeah. Maybe he'd finally started to wonder if River was right and he could be worth a damn. The two most beautiful faces he'd ever seen were in the audience...for *him*. River and Marcy were there tonight because he meant *something* to them. Didn't he owe it to them to think better of himself? Otherwise he did them a disservice—and he couldn't abide that.

Oh God, how long did he have to sit there? Colonel Moriarty had started talking, but Vaughn only wanted to hear River's voice in his ear. Needed it like a parched wasteland needed rain. Marcy waved at him from their place in the third row, and Vaughn very nearly jumped off the stage, ready to take his two girls home. Ready to feed them and put them to sleep and be responsible for them. Forever.

When Vaughn heard his name called, he stood, moving to the podium, saluting as the medal was pinned to his chest. Hell, until that moment, none of this formal shit had meant a thing to Vaughn, but knowing his daughter—and the woman he loved—were watching him receive an honor...that would go with him to his grave as the most unexpected of frozen, perfect moments, even as he remembered the men whose lives were responsible for him being there. For his being alive to remember them at all. Without them, he might have died in that nighttime fight and never returned to River. Never conceived Marcy.

With a silent prayer of thanksgiving, Vaughn took his seat again, trading a look of gravity with River. A look he knew she would interpret correctly to mean, *if I don't get you in my arms soon, doll, I'm going to fade the fuck away.* He knew because she nodded, maybe even feeling the same exact way. One week. In less than a week, his life had become worth living, and he wouldn't take that gift for granted. Never again.

Half an hour later, the ceremony ended with the sound of thundering applause. While the other honorees filed backstage, Vaughn jumped off the front of the elevated area, going straight to River and Marcy, kissing them both on the forehead and hustling them out the back door. By the time they reached the hotel, Marcy's head was lolling to one side in the backseat. After leaving the Pontiac with the valet, they moved in a quiet huddle upstairs to their room, River performing some kind of modern day miracle, unpacking a healthy dinner of roasted turkey and mashed potatoes for Marcy from her overnight bag, heating it in the microwave located in the small kitchenette.

Without prompting, the sleepy child crawled up on Vaughn's lap and ate the meal, her forehead drooping as she chewed. Employing the easiest solution he could muster, Vaughn braced a palm against Marcy's tiny forehead to keep it from landing in the mashed potatoes, sending River into a quiet round of laughter where she observed from one of the double beds.

"What?" He could feel his lopsided grin and didn't care. "It's working."

River acknowledged that with a nod. "So far your list of potential inventions includes a steel cage car seat and forehead strap."

"Just see if I don't follow through, doll," he murmured. "I guess I better get started soon, because if everything goes right, I should be working at the factory starting next week."

River's wide smile wavered. "On the assembly line?"

Vaughn shook his head, trying not to scrutinize her reactions too closely. Was she happy? Disappointed? There was time to figure it out. They had *time*. At least, he was doing his damnedest to hold onto that belief. To say he'd been thrown off by the arrival of River's father was an understatement. But *no*. No, he wouldn't let anyone take away his family again. Never again. Hell, he couldn't live without them now. Couldn't even fathom it. "Uh...not on the line, no. Security." He stabbed a piece of turkey with Marcy's miniature fork, handing it to her. "I went down and spoke to the new owner. He's kind of a dick—" Vaughn winced at his own language, sending River an apologetic look. "But he agreed to meet with me on Monday. I'll be ready. I'm ready now."

Without responding, River stood and moved around the room, hips swaying gently in her modest blue dress, readying one of the beds for Marcy, laying out pajamas that she tugged over the little girl's head a moment later. After suffering through her teeth being brushed, Marcy fell asleep on her stomach, arms and legs sprawled out in four different directions. Vaughn eased the fluffy white comforter over her sleeping form and turned off the light. Then he simply stood there, a mountain range shifting inside his rib cage, the landscape changing forever.

His focus turned on a goddamn dime, though, when River slid her hand into his, tugging him toward the adjoining sitting room. She had to be exaggerating that seductive walk, because God, if her ass moved with any more intention, he'd straight up cry like a baby. His tongue felt thick and useless inside his mouth, his gut tightening as he closed the sliding door behind them.

The room was dark, making the situation illicit as he came up behind River, framing her throat with a hand, riding his other one up her right thigh. "Waiting to have you alone is going to be the hardest part, isn't it?" He lapped at the side of her neck with a starved tongue, needing some of her taste, her scent, her texture. All of it. "Being around you is a hard-on while wearing handcuffs."

"Vaughn...you went and got a job at the factory," she breathed, even as her head tilted to the side. "Why wouldn't you tell me something so important?"

He released an open-mouthed sigh against the flesh he'd dampened. "Maybe I should have." Searching for the right words wasn't easy when he finally had his woman alone. "I want it to be a given that I'm going to bust my ass for us, Riv. But I know it's *not* a given yet. I shouldn't expect that. But I won't stop until it is."

River turned into his hold, gasping as he walked them backward and wedged her up against the far wall. That press of curves and muscle drew strangled groans from both of them, and a distinct resentment for clothing from Vaughn. "Oh my God," River said, a tremor passing through her voice. "It's never going to be any other way, is it? Every single time you touch me…"

"What?" He slanted his mouth over River's in a thoroughly filthy kiss that ended in her thighs trying to climb up his hips. "What's it like? Like you're twice as sensitive than you've ever been? Like every part of you is full and ready to bust the fuck open?"

"Yes." She pushed her tits up like a birthday gift. "Just like that."

"Yeah. We're going to need to work something out, doll. A place to meet on our lunch break. *Something.* You understand?" He slid his left hand up to capture her jaw. "I'm ready to get you back in the habit of three orgasms a day. Morning, afternoon, and night. I'm your fucking meal plan, Riv."

"I'm yours, too." She turned her face, capturing his thumb between her lips, sucking like his digit was providing life-giving sustenance.

With a guttural sound that couldn't be contained, Vaughn rolled his hips against River, giving her a preview of what she had in store—a hungry man who relied on her for survival… and that survival included pleasure only she knew how to give. "Is sucking my thumb your way of saying you'd like to have me for lunch some time?" He coasted one hand down her collarbone, massaging each of her tits in turn, without gentleness, savoring the abrasion of her nipples against his palm. "You want me to send you back to work licking those fuck-me-Vaughn lips?"

She nodded, sliding her mouth up to the tip of his thumb, teasing it with a flickering tongue. "There's another way you want to send me back to work," she whispered, and—*son of a bitch*—his cock stiffened to the point of agony.

"Oh yeah, doll?" Vaughn rubbed his wet thumb along her full upper lip. "How's that?"

"Sore," she said softly, her eyelids drooping, breath coming faster. "You used to send me to school that way, so sitting down would make me think of you."

Christ. How had that memory been shuffled to the back? He recalled it now and reveled in the fresh surge of lust it inspired. Lust and…a tinge of self-hatred. "Ah, Riv. I'm sorry." He lifted desperate fingers to her dress, undoing the buttons fast as he could move them, sliding hands inside the material to grip her tits. "I shouldn't have taken it so hard on you. I just…I couldn't see inside those brick walls and fuck, I couldn't lose you, even though I deserved to. That was the only way I could think to stay with you during the day."

"You did." Her touch landed on his belt buckle, tugging leather through pant loops with a sensual, slithering sound. "You're forgetting how much I begged for it. I needed you with me, too." Soul-punching eyes lifted to his. "I still do."

Vaughn took over the task of unzipping his fly, shoving down his boxers to take out his cock, with a choked curse letting the weight of it bob. "Are you trying to remind me of what I said?" He jerked up the skirt of River's dress, bunching it around her hips. "Did you think I'd forget my promise— that next time would be a rough fuck from behind?"

River's stomach hollowed against his knuckles and

shuddered back out. "I guess you didn't."

"No." He twisted the front of her panties, *tight, tight, tighter.* "You see that couch over there?"

Looking so goddamn beautiful with her perked-up tits lifting and falling, his big hand wrestling with her underwear, dress halfway to the ground, River didn't seem capable of answering, giving a jerky nod instead.

"I've been picturing you face down, with your hips braced on the sofa arm. Ankles spread. Been picturing it for hours." He tugged the panties down, finally giving Vaughn his first sighting of River's sweet-tasting pussy since yesterday. *Hallelujah.* "Knowing you'll be bent over, lifting that ass for me? It had me so hard, my dick kept pushing out through the opening of my shorts, chafing against the inside of my clothes. All motherfucking night. So, no, I didn't forget. I've been trying to calm myself down enough that I don't break the furniture trying to abuse your G-spot."

"Stop," she moaned shakily.

Vaughn leaned down to get in her face, their lips brushing together. "Stop what?"

"Trying to calm down." Her gaze raked down his body. "This hero gets what he wants tonight."

"I only care about being your hero," he rasped.

"You always have been."

That was the only encouragement Vaughn needed to spur River toward the couch, positioning her body the way he'd been imagining. Ass cheeks, smooth as silk, pushed up like dual hills of hotness, her pussy—shining with moisture—peeking out between them. Her ankles weren't far enough apart yet, but he knew his woman's game. Knew she got turned on by the slightest aggression on his part. And he was more than happy to oblige her. Hell, he was ripe and ready. His cock was like a fucking monument against his abdomen, weeping from the tip with the need to push into that tight, clinging business he had the nerve to refer to merely as *pussy*. Nah, it was life. Relief. Pleasure. Home. *His.*

"Mine." The single hoarse word was accompanied by the two fingers he slid inside her, easing them deep, rotating, pulling back out, using the dampness he took away to lubricate the condom he rolled down his swollen inches. "Go ahead. Give me that look over your shoulder. You know the one I want."

A visible shudder rippled up her back, but she tossed that blonde hair and turned her head, giving him that beautiful profile, complete with puffy, parted lips. And then she turned a few more degrees, hit him with blue eyes, and slowly shifted her bare ass against his lap. "Come and get it," she whispered.

Vaughn fell over her like a fuck-hungry prison inmate, planting one fist on the couch beside her face, using the other to guide his cock home. A thrust of his hips and he was ensconced in her tight welcome, the hot curve of her ass pressed to his belly. *Christ. Jesus Christ.* Every time with River felt like his very first sex act, pressure mounting in his balls before he could take a single pump. He could see the shocked O of her open mouth as her face was still turned to the side, cheek pressed to the couch cushion. "Same way for you, isn't it? It's like getting your first cock all over again, right, doll?" He tested her heat with a teasing jerk of his hips, forcing a muffled moan from her mouth. "And who was your first?"

"*You were.*"

Vaughn inserted a foot into the center of River's splayed stance, pushing her legs wider, allowing his dick to sink even deeper on gusty, simultaneous sighs. "Tight as the day I broke you in," he whispered into her hair, taking a moment to savor the way their bodies curved over the sofa arm, how much control he had over when and how they moved. How compact and supple she felt beneath him. *Trusting* him. "I didn't think you could get any more important...any more fucking precious to me than you were that day. And then I lived forty-nine months without you."

Eyes clenched shut, Vaughn reared back and drove forward, dropping his face into the crook of River's neck, barely able to withstand the intensity of being inside her again. Of feeling that severed connection joining, repairing, against odds that had been stacked a mile high. Their fisted hands moved closer, closer, until they were joined together on the cushion, fused as one, same as their lower bodies.

"Squeeze my hand when I hit your spot," Vaughn ordered, sounding as if his vocal chords were being strangled. He loosened his buttock muscles, allowing his achy cock to slip mostly free, before tightening them on a deep drive, pushing from his feet for extra leverage, ramming River's hips up against the couch's arm. When she moaned a string of unintelligible words, fingers attempting to crush his, Vaughn knew exactly what she meant. "Smacked right up against it, didn't I?" He gave her another rough pound, loving the sound of flesh bumping flesh, his balls swinging up to reacquaint themselves with River's underside. "Fuck. You hear that little slapping sound? If I jerk myself off with enough soap in the shower, I can almost recreate it. Almost. But never just as perfect. Nothing is that sweet and perfect." The tempo of his pumps increased out of necessity, a storm building in his stomach. "Didn't stop me from trying every chance I got, did it, doll? Imagining you taking me, hard as I could give it, getting slapped with my flesh as a reward for being brave."

River released a long moan into the sofa, her shoulders beginning to fill with tension, her back arching against his chest. "Vaughn, please. Vaughn, please."

"Tell me when you're close, and I'll drill that spot, Riv." His mouth was making a mess out of her hair, rummaging through it, breathing through the fragrant strands. "My cock hurts from missing you, wants to coat you. Just let me get you a little closer so I don't leave you behind."

To anyone else, he might not be making sense, but River's head bobbed, hand tightening in his grip. "I'm…just a little harder. Harder."

Vaughn could feel the mask of pure agony take over his face, as he obliged his woman's needs—needs he would have walked over a barren desert full of live mines to fulfill. The stiff couch arm kept River from budging—not even a centimeter—as he quickened his pace, grunts punctuating the air now. Sweat rolling down the sides of his face. The furniture scuffed on the floor, lifting up and banging back down against the carpeted floor with coarse thuds. "How close, how close, how close," he chanted, his teeth skimming up and down her neck, over her damp shoulders. Both hands slipped beneath her body, palming her tits and tweaking the stiff nipples, showing them no mercy. "It's going to sting when you clean yourself in the shower tomorrow morning. Every fucking morning from now on. And I want you to tell me all about it. Get mad at me, get turned on. Just tell me how your pussy feels the morning after I fuck it. That's my privilege, you hear me?"

"*Yes*," River gasped. "Close, I'm really close."

Vaughn dropped his hand from River's tits before delivering a sharp spank to both nipples, the smooth undersides of her bouncing orbs. Then harder, with more force, as his dick pinned her with brutal thrusts to the elevated couch arm. "Watch me over that shoulder. Show me how you look at your man."

He could tell it was an effort for River to focus on him, but that line of invisible wire between them was a requirement. It heated and glowed as his hips reached their peak speed, leaving and filling so fast, the sound of smacking blurred together in a continuous, filthy noise. *Smacksmacksmacksmack*.

And the climax hurtling toward him brought uncontrolled

speech to his lips, aggression to his hands and pummeling body. "You never stopped being mine. I need you...mine. *River.* It hurts and it feels so fucking good." He twisted his fingers in her hair and pulled. "Keep your goddamn thighs *open.*"

The moment her pussy seized around him, Vaughn's muscle control vanished, leaving his upper half draped over River as his hips gave their final, uneven drives, pleasure flooding out and shaking him to the core of his being, finally leaving him replete. At some point, his arms had banded beneath River, holding her steady as their heartbeats eventually slowed.

"I know we can't sleep in the same bed yet," he said against her shoulder. "But...just let me hold you here a while, huh?"

When she nodded, he blew out the breath he'd been holding and laid them down on the couch, turning River so she could tuck her head beneath his chin, feet between his calves. The smoothness of her palms traced up and down through his chest hair, and God, the world finally made sense again in that moment. "Thank you for coming with me. Seeing you and Marcy in the crowd..."

After a beat, River spoke into the hanging silence. "That man you were on the stage today...that hero. That's how I always saw you." She laid a kiss in the center of his chest. "I just hope you see yourself that way now."

Vaughn hooked the arm River was using as a headrest and crooked the elbow behind her neck, crushing her close, lips lingering on her forehead. Speaking was too difficult, so he used his breath, his mouth in her hair to show her what he couldn't say out loud, hoping all the while that her faith, teamed with his unshakable love, would be enough to keep them from breaking apart again. Because not everyone saw him as the man who'd been honored that night. Some people—namely River's father—would only ever see him as gutter trash that had no place beside River. There was a test coming, Vaughn could feel it. He just hoped his burgeoning self-worth—still tenuous at best—would be enough to withstand whatever came their way. It had to be. Because if he lost River twice, he might as well have died back on the battlefield.

"Vaughn?" River's breath drifted over his throat. "You've gone all tense on me."

He forced his muscles to relax. "I'm just thinking about how much I hate sleeping without you."

She nuzzled her face beneath his chin. "Soon."

Please God. Let that be the case.

Chapter Eighteen

River woke before Marcy—a first—due to a relentless buzz saw whirring at the back of her skull. She couldn't quite give a name to what was causing the anxiety, only knew the idea of returning to Hook didn't bring the sense of comfort it should. Guilt crept in when an image of her father rose like a harbinger. She shouldn't feel that way about the man who'd raised her. He was a good man who cared for his family. But something was off. *Just a quick call to check in…and I'll feel better.*

With Vaughn asleep in the second room, door closed, River unhooked her cell phone from the charger and snuck out into the hallway. Knowing her father would be on the fishing trip, she dialed his mobile, frowning when it went to voicemail. After leaving a quick message to return her call, River resolved to try him again later. Just as she turned to reenter the room, Vaughn appeared in the doorway, barefoot in low-slung jeans. "Hey." He nodded at the phone, completely unaware he'd spiked her libido like a football. "Who're you calling?"

Why did she have this sudden sense of being…disloyal? It was ridiculous. Wasn't it? "My father." She lowered her voice in deference to their sleeping child. "He's staying with us a couple of nights while he's on a fishing trip. I just wanted to let him know we were coming home. In case he'd returned early."

Vaughn's expression was carved in stone. "Why didn't you tell me he was in Hook?"

The buzzing increased, making her skin feel tight. "I don't know," she whispered, wondering for the first time if Vaughn could possibly fill in the blanks.

River wanted to ignore the anxiety that formed a barrier around Vaughn as they drove back into Hook an hour later. After the soul-squeezing sex they'd shared last night, and the transition into family life this morning, she'd forgotten to worry, positive she'd imagined the lines around his mouth when they'd returned from the hallway. There was nothing imaginary about the way he continued to rake agitated fingers though his hair now, though, answering her in monosyllables.

This pattern was too familiar, even after so much time having passed. Vaughn clamming up, neglecting to make eye contact. River getting anxious, withdrawing into her head to overanalyze, wondering where they'd taken a wrong turn. In her early twenties, she would have remained in that holding pattern until Vaughn broke her out of it. But she'd grown up, and she could do that for herself now.

When he coasted to a stop at a red light, blocks from her house, River reached over, laying a hand on his knee. "Your meeting at the factory is tomorrow. Do you need help preparing…or anything?"

"It's under control," he answered, barely moving his lips. But he seemed to realize with a double take how short he'd been throughout the last few miles. "I've, uh… I've been contacting men, mostly guys from the area who Duke and I went through basic training with. They haven't had the easiest time finding employment, and they needed a chance like this."

River glanced through the windshield with a dazed smile. "Wow. The factory is going to be guarded by ex-military. Can't say we won't be safe."

Instead of laughing, the way she'd hoped, Vaughn's jaw went tight. "Not like before, right? When you were working in that shit stack during the day and coming home in the pitch black—*alone*—after serving drinks in the bar. You weren't safe then, were you, Riv?"

She slowly took her hand back. "Why are you bringing this up now?" Her sternum ached, as if she'd been struck by a fastball, right in the center. "I thought we were moving past this—"

"Sometimes the past doesn't let you off that easy," he gritted out. In the backseat, Marcy started crying, and Vaughn's face paled, his attention flying to the rearview mirror. "I thought she was asleep, I—"

"It's fine," River interrupted, her own irritation rising. She took off her seat belt, turning around in the passenger seat on her knees. All was well as soon as she handed Marcy a juice box, but Vaughn? Not so much. His eyes were back on the road, harder to read than before. And it speared her with dread. Had he changed his mind about them getting back together? She didn't think it possible, not after the bond they'd proven last night was still undeniably intact. But... what if she was wrong?

In that moment of doubt, River learned something about herself. The possibility of Vaughn having second thoughts didn't make her want to fall down, dissolving into a puddle of tears, like the girl she'd been at twenty-two. No, it made her want to fight. For them? Yes. Just not that second. She was too pissed off at having their trip brought to a crappy end. For having her fear of Vaughn leaving tugged to the surface. And most of all for the reminder how quickly he could still make her insecure with his silence.

As soon as Vaughn pulled the Pontiac to a stop, River pushed open her door, slammed it, and hit the sidewalk, taking Marcy out of her car seat with a smile she hoped was patient and unfazed. *Yeah, right.*

"Hey," Vaughn said from behind her, having the absolute nerve to sound baffled. "What are you stomping around about?"

She took a deep breath and faced Vaughn, forcing herself to keep her voice down. "I want you to leave. Now, please."

His hands went to his hips, dark eyebrows drawing together. "Why is that?"

"Because you're being a jerk," she responded succinctly. "And you're not going to talk about *why*. You're just going to stew. Or be cryptic and says things like, 'sometimes the past doesn't let you off that easy, little lady.'" He narrowed his eyes at the way River mimicked his deep voice, but she didn't give him time to respond. "Well, no kidding. No kidding. Don't talk to me like I haven't figured that out."

He took a step closer. "Doll—"

"Oh no. Don't doll me." She put up a hand, halting his progress in her direction. "You want to be a part of us? Stop being such a mystery. There's no room for that here. We need to be on the same page to be a team, like we spoke about. So until you get there? Please. Leave."

"Not leaving when you're this mad." He scratched the side of his stubbled jaw, running his gaze up and down her body. "Actually, I don't think I've ever seen you this mad."

"If you tell me it's turning you on, I'm going to slug you right in the stomach."

"All right," he said, voice getting harder. "I won't tell you. But you should know I'm thinking it."

River's foot ached with the need to stomp. She and Vaughn were squared off, having moved closer when she obviously hadn't been paying attention. *Dammit*, she hated that the argument was only half the reason her blood grew hot, her skin turning sensitive beneath the dress she wore. Beneath his white shirt, she could make out the outline of the unrefined tattoo forming her name and longed to trace it with her fingertips, kiss each letter. *God.* How could she want to scratch his eyes out and jump him at the same time?

"They're back!"

The familiar voice caught River and Vaughn off guard, both of them twisting in the newcomer's direction. Half a block down, Duke's four sisters were headed in their direction, waving with their free hands, the other hands holding bags from the local toy store.

"What is happening here?" Vaughn muttered the question on River's mind, just as Marcy started to kick up a fuss for being left in her car seat too long. Automatically, River went to work, freeing the three-year-old and setting her on the sidewalk, which set off a fit of squealing from the sister posse now even with River's front yard.

"Duke said you ought to be home about now."

"Just stopping by with a few things for the little one."

"Lisa cuts hair. Does the kid need a haircut? She brought her scissors. Good ones. You can't get them just anywhere."

"How was traffic?"

No one waited for an answer to that last question, all four sisters hustling a dazzled—and somewhat dazed—Marcy inside, somehow knowing exactly where River hid the spare key inside the decorative lantern arrangement.

After a moment River looked at Vaughn. "What just happened?"

A corner of his mouth edged up. "I think Duke needed to watch SportsCenter."

"I'm never getting rid of them now, am I?"

"We." He was back to sounding irritable. *"We're* never

getting rid of them."

His unwise tone of voice snapped River's spine straight. "I meant what I said, Vaughn," she said. "I can't do this—us— if you're going to leave me wondering what's coming. I need to *know* what's coming." *Way to be clear, River.* "I need to not be worried I'm losing you again. And *damn* you for making me feel that way."

Vaughn plowed forward, pinning River to the car, his hands tunneling through her hair, his body hard, *so hard*, against her own. "Losing me? God, what made you think that? What did I do to make you think you could"—his touch dropped away like his muscles had given out—"lose me."

She watched the irony of that question register in Vaughn's eyes, but didn't feel any victory in it. Only relief at having gotten through, of not being alone in the shell of her constant worry. "We can't get by on just sex anymore." Even as she spoke the sentiment, even fully meaning it, her tummy flipped at saying the word "sex" when Vaughn's mouth was only a breath away. He liked hearing River say it, too. She knew by the *tick-tick-tick* in his cheek. "I like that we communicate that way, but we need words, too. I need words and honesty. All the time. You can't disappear into yourself on me. I get scared, and I've gotten too strong to feel that way."

Head dipped forward, Vaughn settled a hand at her waist. "I scare you, Riv?" He started to talk, stopped, started again. "Jesus, doll. You know I'd rather die than make you scared, don't you?"

"You don't do it on purpose," she whispered, hating the misery in his voice. "I know you wouldn't. But I can already feel us slipping backward, and I won't let it happen. You have to *talk* to me."

Vaughn's thumb began to strum her belly in a way she knew wasn't conscious, but it sent shimmering lust right to her center. Made everything hidden by her panties feel heavy.

Achy. "You're the only one I've ever talked to. The years I spent out of Hook? Sometimes I went days without saying a word. Why the hell would I say something you couldn't hear, you know?"

With a vigorous twist taking place in her chest, River curled a hand in the bottom of Vaughn's T-shirt, pulling him closer. "You told me about what happened in Afghanistan. I know it was hard, but you did it." She went up on her toes and kissed his chin. "Tell me what's bothering you now, and we'll work through it together."

Against her lips, she felt Vaughn's jaw harden, and knew they'd hit an impasse. "I can't change overnight, Riv. Some things are better left unsaid."

She rocked back on her heels. "There you go being cryptic again."

"I'm not leaving Hook. Not leaving you. That's written in stone," he grated, pressing her up against the car, frustration echoing through his big body, making hers sing nonetheless. "Let me take you somewhere. I'll remind you of the way we work. One of us gets bent out of shape, and the other one smooths it out."

"That's how we used to work," River breathed, trapping a moan in her throat when Vaughn dipped his head to capture her earlobe with his teeth. "I love that part of us. But I'll go crazy without more." With a will she hadn't been aware of possessing, River slipped out from beneath Vaughn's crowding frame. "Figure out if you can give it to me."

She walked into the house on unsteady legs, feeling Vaughn's gaze on her the whole time. But she didn't look back, because he would see her susceptibility. And River wouldn't allow that after the battle she'd just fought. The battle for *them*.

Chapter Nineteen

When Vaughn pulled up outside the motel, he couldn't remember the drive over. He'd replayed the conversation with River so many times, he'd started saying the words out loud, responding with shit he *should* have said back outside the house. Apart from that one time he'd blown off dinner with her parents, he'd never seen River that pissed off. And yeah, that display of temper had gotten his dick hard, because he knew she'd put up *just enough* resistance in the process of getting her clothes off, the way she'd done that night on his kitchen floor so long ago.

But he hadn't expected *actual* resistance. As in, "learn to communicate or go the hell home, asshole."

The worst damn part of it? River was right. He doled out just enough of his thoughts to get what he wanted from people. But employing that same method of distance-keeping with River had been a big, shortsighted mistake. A mistake he'd been making since they'd gotten together as teenagers. One he didn't have a damn clue how to correct, and one that couldn't be blurred or ignored with sex.

Before she'd left him standing there gaping after her on the curb, she'd praised him for opening up about his experience overseas. Now he felt sick about letting her think he'd been honest for honesty's sake. No, it had only been another instance of him doling out the truth. Telling River her father had given him no choice but to leave Hook—the *actual* reason behind his disappearing—would hurt her in an unimaginable way. And wasn't that the reason he kept things from River to begin with? Saving her from feeling doubt or pain...or worse—the need to give him sympathy when comfort was something he didn't understand.

There hadn't been comfort for him growing up, only distractions. Well, that shit wasn't going to fly anymore. By coaxing River into bed every time she tried to make things personal, he was actually pushing her away. The absolute last thing he ever wanted. Hell, being near her was the *only* thing worth fighting for in this life, but he'd been battling against himself.

Time to change that. Time to shatter the solo comfort zone he'd been living in and build it around his family instead. Unfortunately, doing so could sever the bond between River and the family who'd raised her, loved her, and helped her pick up the pieces when he bailed. Was he ready for that?

Vaughn climbed out of his truck and stopped, lifting an eyebrow at the polished black Mercedes parked in the motel lot. Identifying the vehicle didn't take a private investigator, being that only one man in Hook owned a ride like that—Renner Bastion, the new factory owner. Vaughn wondered if the guy might be closed up in one of the rooms, working through some afternoon delight, but quickly disregarded the notion. Renner wouldn't sully himself with the stink of ancient polyester.

His theory was proven correct when he caught sight of suit-and-tie dressed Renner waiting outside his door, speaking briskly into his cell phone. But he ended the call when he saw Vaughn approaching. "Mr. De Matteo. Are you always this difficult to reach?"

Interesting question. River would have answered it with a resounding yes. "Depends on who you're asking."

"I'd point out that I was asking you, but I don't have time to talk in circles." Renner made a quick adjustment of his tie clip. "I've been called out of town, so I won't be available for our meeting tomorrow."

Vaughn's stomach twisted. "You came to tell me this in person?"

"No, I came to have the meeting now." For the first time, Vaughn noticed how stressed out Renner looked, lines prominent around his eyes and mouth. Maybe not quite as flawless under all the expensive nonsense he was wearing? "There was a break-in yesterday at the factory and a new piece of equipment—just delivered—was stolen. Had to be someone who knew the delivery was coming, which unfortunately, could have been four dozen construction workers, who I didn't have time to vet and certainly can't take time to question." A brisk roll of his shoulders. "I'm beginning to see the merit in a twenty-four-hour security team."

Hope replaced the dread in Vaughn's middle, spurring on a sense of urgency. This was his shot. While his head was still preoccupied with River, focusing now could mean good things for the family he needed to win back. For good. Forever. "We going to do this out here, or you want to come inside?"

There was a flash of something speculative in Renner's expression—reserved, but *there*, nonetheless—and enough to make Vaughn wonder if Renner might have heard that same line from men before, with far different intentions. "No. Outside will do," the factory owner finally answered, after clearing his throat. "I conduct *all* my business meetings in shitty parking lots. Can't you tell?"

When Vaughn laughed, the other man looked somewhat startled. "Fair enough." He blew out a breath, recalling the system he'd laid out in his mind. "As I mentioned before, you need a night patrol with two guards, one in the control room, one walking the four perimeters." Using as much detail as he could, Vaughn explained the sophisticated monitoring system he had in mind, one he'd installed and operated at his job while living in Baltimore. "But it's not just security on the outside you need to think about. I love the people in this town, but you can't have blind faith when money is involved. Once you have human resources in place, we can work with them to arrange a security check as the employees leave the premises each day. I'd also prohibit any photography and—"

"Right. I'm relieved you've put some thought into this." Renner checked something on his cell phone screen. "I wasn't sure what to expect."

Vaughn grinned. "You were worried I was going to show up with some binoculars and a six pack. Happy to prove you wrong." He tossed his car keys up in the air and caught them. "As of now, I've got one man on board. Milo Bautista. We were overseas together, and he's been doing security…of a kind…up in Boston. Little rough around the edges, but he takes his jobs seriously. He'll help me train the new hires."

Renner considered him a moment before removing a business card from his front pocket and handing it over to Vaughn. "You'll need to speak to my accountant about putting funds in place. And I'll want to meet this partner of yours when I'm back in town." He gave a firm nod as he strode past Vaughn toward the black luxury vehicle. "Congratulations. You're hired."

Hot damn. Even while going through his whole spiel, he hadn't been sure of the outcome. The opportunity seemed too easy for someone who'd fought for every chance he'd ever been given. "Thank you," Vaughn called, without turning around.

A car door opened behind Vaughn. "One question, Mr. De Matteo. If you show up to my factory in ripped jeans, who is going to escort *you* out?"

Vaughn snorted, turning to watch the Mercedes pull out of the lot. His chest was so packed full of relief and anticipation and leftover nerves that when he attempted to enter his room, he stopped.

His truck burned rubber onto the road a moment later, words—long overdue words—he needed to say to River fighting for room in his throat. And maybe for the first time in his life he felt capable of backing up the promises he planned to make.

Chapter Twenty

River had just set Marcy up at the dining room table with her lunch—Duke's sisters on all sides, nursing cups of coffee—when Vaughn's truck screeched to a stop at the curb. From the house's front window, she watched him alight from the driver's side, that long-legged stride eating up the walkway leading to her front door. Maybe intuition was to blame for the bubble of excitement that lifted, bumping off her ribs before rising to her throat. A sense of…magic in the air. Which would sound crazy if she spoke it out loud, but made sense when kept contained inside her whirring thoughts.

It was the only other time River could recall Vaughn moving with that much purpose, save the instances he'd been racing toward a fight. The first time he'd said I love you, River—age seventeen—had already said it first. While making out in the back of his truck, hidden inside fogged up windows, she'd whispered it in his ear. *I love you, Vaughn.* God, he'd looked horrified, diving out through the back door, climbing into the driver's seat and taking River home. Not even bothering to say a word as she ran toward the house…

River could barely see through eyes made puffy by crying. After Vaughn dropped her off, she'd fallen across her bed, not bothering to muffle the sounds of misery coming from her mouth, since nobody was home to hear them. At first, she swore the pounding on the downstairs front door was her damaged heart, finally giving up the battle. Until it got louder, and louder, then stopped, right before a crash sent her jackknifing on the mattress, staring at her bedroom door, positive an intruder would burst through and kill her, officially making that day the worst in history.

But it wasn't an intruder who'd sent her door slamming against the opposite wall. It was Vaughn—eyes wild, breath labored, hands bloody from pounding on her front door. He took one look at her tear-stained face and dove forward, tackling her onto the bed. "I love you, I love you, I love you. Okay? Okay, doll? I'm the worst fuck-up in the world, and I shouldn't let you love me." His voice was hoarse and agonized. "It's the best thing that ever happened to me. And I'm the worst thing that ever happened to you. But I can't help loving you so much. I can't help needing you this bad."

It was like an abrupt ending to the worst storm in history, perfect sunshine breaking through the clouds to shine down on River's heart. Healing it, healing her. *She wrapped her legs around Vaughn's waist and let his mouth remove the tears from her face with kisses, laughing in a way that sounded sad, but was really so happy she'd never heard the like coming from her own lips. "Vaughn, why would you say something like that about yourself—"*

Her words ended on a gasp, when Vaughn thrust his hips between her thighs, jolting River's body on the bed. "Can we play one of our games, Riv?" His tongue teased the flesh beneath her ear. "You're so sweet, you make me ache all over.

You aching for me, too, doll?"

Another desperate rocking of bodies, private parts grinding together. The new, sexual energy she still hadn't grown accustom to blocked out her frustration over Vaughn not answering her question. It had been important, right? "Yes, I ache."

"We can't have that." The heel of his hand pressed against the sensitive spot hidden beneath her skirt, her panties. "Let me play with you here, where I showed you it feels good."

"What about you?" she breathed, her spine curving under the onslaught of sensation. Oh...wow. Oh wow. He was so good at everything.

His knees planted on either side of her right leg, his erection pressing and sliding up and down her thigh. "These legs don't open for no one but me...knowing that...rubbing against them while I tease your pussy..." His groan raised goose bumps on River's arms. "Aw, Christ. That's going to be enough to drain me."

For the next half hour, their groans increased in fervor, mouths sliding together, River's heart expanding until she wasn't sure she could stand it. It wasn't until Vaughn left much later that River realized he'd never answered her question.

Now, with four women in her kitchen drinking coffee and discussing the merits of a Myrtle Beach timeshare, River could tell Vaughn had something to say. She was simultaneously terrified and anxious beyond belief to hear it. The women seemed to sense something interesting was afoot because their chatter cut off, just in time for Vaughn to pound heavily on the door. Even having expected his knock, River jumped, hand flying to her heart.

"Who's there?" Marcy singsonged from the table, around a mouthful of grilled cheese. "Is it daddy?"

The pounding started again as River reached the door, finally ceasing when she unlocked it and slowly pulled it open. Oh…*oh*, apparently she would never get used to the beauty of Vaughn's vulnerable side. The evidence flipped her stomach over like a fried egg, sizzling in that certainty. His muscles stood out against the front of his T-shirt, his big, capable hands flexing at his sides. "I got the job," he murmured. "Security for the factory. He hired me."

In an instant, everything that happened that morning *poofed* into a cloud of dust, making way for a rush of pride so thick she couldn't speak. They were no longer two arguing adults with years of pain on their backs. They were just River and Vaughn, curled up inside his leather jacket, listening to the rain patter onto the roof of his truck. She stood there, hands fluttering with an attempt to communicate her happiness, before she simply threw herself at Vaughn where he still stood on the porch. "I knew he would. Why wouldn't he want someone like you? I knew."

Vaughn caught her wrists and eased her away, fire burning in his eyes. "I'm happy, too, Riv. I'm happy because now I can help support my family the way I need. The way *we* need." His throat worked with a swallow. "But here's the thing, okay? Here's the thing. You're the only one who ever knew I was capable of…*anything*. If I'd let myself believe you and I'd failed, it would have killed me." He shook his head. "But I was doing you a disservice, doll. Because if you loved me, I'd already won the world. You see?"

River's arms went limp, dropping from Vaughn's grip, before he picked them back up and rested them on his shoulders, as if he required them to keep going.

"All the times I've been quiet, all the times I might slip and be too quiet in the future, I'm just thinking of ways to keep you. Okay, dammit, River? It's all I ever think about. Even when I was gone, my brain played the *what if* game. What if she's crying and needs me? What if I just climbed back into her window *right now*? Would she let me stand there and look at her?"

River didn't think she could take any more bald, beautiful honesty all at once, but Vaughn plowed on as if he didn't know how to cap the flow once it started. "No more *what ifs*, Riv. I *need* you. I need my family. If that means saying whatever crazy bullshit is on my mind, so be it. On the way home, I was listing all the ways you could get taken away from me. And how I could combat them. Okay? That's all I got."

Ignoring the chorus of feminine sighs coming from the kitchen, she lunged into his hold, pressing and holding her open lips against his neck, attempting to slow her racing pulse. No dice. It rattled on, shaking her body until she felt like a fizzing soda ready to blow its top. "W-why…how could I get taken away from you?"

Vaughn remained silent a moment. "I was in such a bad way that night, Riv. When I left Hook…and you. There was a lot of ugly in my head." His hand curved to the back of her skull, tugging her into the crook of his neck. "But I was going to you. I was never going to let go, until—"

"Sorry to interrupt."

It took River a few beats to recognize her father's voice, coming from the porch behind Vaughn. She cracked the lids of her eyes, taking in the tips of his fishing poles, the unreadable expression on his face. River loved her father like crazy, but in that moment, she wanted him gone, not only because she suspected Vaughn had been ready to shed light on that night at the motel, but because she could feel the stiffness pervading Vaughn's muscles. Could feel him shutting down inside her hold.

"Dad," River said finally, stepping back but taking hold of Vaughn's hand, some intuition telling her it was necessary. "You're back. Come on in."

"Mr. Purcell." Vaughn eased aside, allowing her father to enter the house and set down his fishing equipment. "How were the fish biting?"

"Not as well as they were here, I see." Her father laughed at his own joke, but no one joined him. "I could use some help bringing in the rest of my gear. Vaughn?"

Wishing away the sense of dread, River moved forward. "I can do it," she said, doing a double take when Vaughn let go of her hand.

"I got it," Vaughn said quickly, giving her what might have been meant as a reassuring look, but it didn't come close to accomplishing the task. Her father and Vaughn walked down the steps without speaking, as she looked on, feeling more in the dark than ever.

Chapter Twenty-One

Vaughn looked down into the empty trunk of River's father's car and braced himself for whatever was coming. He could feel River watching from the front window, so he pasted a casual smile on his face. And waited.

Goddammit. Throughout his entire life, Vaughn had given the middle finger to anyone who tried to get in his way. Except for this man. This man who'd cost him forty-nine months of being with the love of his life. This man who'd cost him the experience of his daughter's first steps, first tooth, first haircut. Why? Why had he allowed River's father to dictate his decisions, when he would normally have fought any other son of a bitch who presumed to do the same?

He'd just answered his own question. It was *River's* father. And Vaughn knew what living without family felt like, knew the absence presented itself at the oddest times. Sitting in a diner on Sunday morning, watching families eat pancakes. Or stepping aside to let a family in identical sports jerseys pass on the sidewalk. Yeah. Vaughn knew all about that void, and saving River that pain—*any* pain—had been his reason for allowing Mr. Purcell to tread on him. For River's sake.

Now, with River's worried gaze tracking his movements, that pattern swallowed him up, forced him to nod respectfully at the man he should hate. Hell, maybe he did. Maybe he hated him more than the devil.

"I have to say, I'm surprised," Mr. Purcell began. "I didn't think you'd come back for Marcy. Thought knowing about her would keep you gone, actually."

Sickness invaded Vaughn's stomach at the thought of shirking a responsibility he celebrated. "I guess that's proof you don't know me very well."

The older man's smile pulled tight. "Maybe you're not as big a coward as your father, but if I remember correctly, you only need a little urging to get gone."

"A *little* urging?" Hearing the ire in his voice, Vaughn closed his eyes and took a long, fortifying breath. Sensing there was another axe about to drop, Vaughn delayed the inevitable by asking the question that had been plaguing him since childhood. "What happened between you and my father?"

River's father's mouth twisted, as if the mere mention of Vaughn's father disgusted him. "Never told you, did he? I guess you were too young when he split to understand, anyway." Vaughn ignored the pang in his stomach. "I had a full ride scholarship to Rutgers. Football. I was getting out of this fucking town. And your father—who was supposed to be my teammate—hated me for it. His only options were the factory, or being broke in some other shitty place."

Vaughn watched as River's father yanked up his pant leg, indicating a surgery scar on his right knee.

"He did this. Last practice of the season, he took a cheap shot at me after the whistle. *Your* father." His pointed a shaking finger at Vaughn but was obviously being careful to keep his back turned toward the house, making their conversation seem run-of-the-mill. "I watched you turn into a loser, just like him. Vandalizing property, stealing cars, walking around with a chip on your shoulder. And then you started seeing my daughter."

Usually when facts fell into place for Vaughn, he appreciated the sense of understanding, but this wasn't one of those times. His gut felt pumped full of lead as he saw the situation through the eyes of River's father. Of course he would hate Vaughn for being the one to keep River from attending college. It must have been like déjà vu. A new generation of De Matteo keeping his daughter from fulfilling her potential. Jesus Christ, he felt ill. If he'd been alone, he would have sunk down onto the curb. "I wanted her to go. I—"

"You didn't try hard enough, though. Did you? All those times you were in my house at night. You think I didn't know?"

"Why didn't you come throw me out?" The words stung leaving his mouth. "I would have gone. I would've known you were right."

The older man stared off down the block, as if seeing into the past. "She would have only gone after you, twice as hard. And you would have been back the next day. I needed you to…"

"Break her heart?" Vaughn's hands twitched with the need to ball into fists. "I did. And it was the worst decision I've ever made. I'll pay for it the rest of my life whenever she looks worried I'll do it again."

"But you will." Mr. Purcell's disgust had returned. "You'll do it again, whether it's today or next year. Might as well save some time."

Here it comes. Vaughn's pulse shot into overdrive as the older man opened a compartment inside the trunk and removed a stack of papers.

"I never transferred the deed, Vaughn." The silence

following that statement was so complete, Vaughn could hear his heartbeat slow, slow, until it almost stopped. "When River announced she was pregnant, I made the decision. The baby meant a connection between you two, and if she ever got in touch…if you ever came back to Hook, I couldn't risk the man who cost my daughter her future living inside my house. I can't *abide* it."

"So what's the play?" Vaughn's body was exhausted, so exhausted. Like he'd just climbed a mountain. "If I stay, you take the house away? You would do that to your granddaughter?"

River's father had the decency to turn red, but it was half anger. "You going to stick around to find out?" He shook his head. "I don't think so. You can't chance it when I've proven what I'll do to keep you out of her life."

You can't.

Those two words sent steam rising in his belly, heating insides that had gone cold. Vaughn longed to embrace that kindled fire—the reminder of his fighter nature—then he thought of his bank account. How the money it contained was honest and hard earned, but still not enough to give River and Marcy the kind of place they were used to. Not enough to come close.

Painfully conscious of River's attention on him, Vaughn backed away from the piece of paper that had dictated so much of his life, and strode toward his truck, his legs weighing a thousand pounds each. With a loud clanging resonating in his ears, Vaughn got behind the wheel and drove.

• • •

River flung open the front door of her house, running down the pathway at breakneck speed. "Vaughn!"

Oh God. She should have left the house sooner. Why had

she just stood there, frozen in place by the window, hoping for some kind of resolution between her father and Vaughn when it was so obvious a bond would never form? Stupid, so stupid. And now he was gone. The man who'd so recently opened himself up, on the verge of more, had been shut down. She'd watched it happen. Unbelievably, it had been her father to finally pull the plug.

"What did you say to him?"

Her father turned, looking wearier than she'd ever seen him. "Nothing he hasn't heard before."

"What does that *mean*?" River screamed the words through her teeth. "I'm tired of being treated like a child who can't handle hearing truth, or making her own decisions. Answer me like a goddamn adult."

When he only turned toward his car, muttering under his breath, River snatched the piece of paper he was holding out of his hand. It was familiar. She had the same document inside a file folder inside her bedroom closet, along with Marcy's birth certificate and her high school diploma. But something was different about this deed…it didn't have her name on it. Anywhere. Only her father's name. "What is this? The old deed?" He didn't answer. "Why do you have it out?"

"No reason," he answered firmly, reaching out to take it back. But River jerked it away, discomfort settling on her shoulders. "Let's go inside, River."

"Yes." Turning on a heel, she continued to scrutinize the deed. Same dates. Same handwriting. Same everything. The only thing different was the name. When River looked up again, she was halfway up the staircase to her bedroom. From below, her father called her name, but she ignored him, continuing to ascend and walking straight into her closet. A moment later, she had the deeds side by side, examining them with growing dread—dread she didn't fully understand yet, but it dragged her down, down, underneath roaring waves.

"Mine is a copy."

Until her father released a sigh behind her, River hadn't realized he'd followed. She stood, the deed held in a lifeless hand at her side.

"Mine is a copy. Is...did you ever actually transfer the deed?" She held the papers up to her face, paying close attention to the name section. "Or did you just white out your name, make a copy...and type mine in? This was never filed, was it?" As she remembered Vaughn's white face as he stumbled toward the truck, River's body started to shake. "What does Vaughn have to do with any of this?"

Her father rubbed his eyes with a thumb and index finger. Waiting silently for him to speak was difficult, but she was also semi-grateful for the reprieve. What was coming? Finally he spoke, his voice so low she could barely make out his words. "No matter how many times I told you he wasn't up to your standards, you didn't listen. You wouldn't listen." His throat worked. "The night he left, we met at the Third Shift. I told him I'd give you the house if he left. He couldn't give you a damn thing, River. This house was all I had to guarantee you didn't throw everything away." The ensuing pause was deafening. "And although the stakes have changed, it still is."

An agonized sound fell from River's lips, pressure mounting behind her eyes. "Still is?" She wrapped her arms around her middle. "I don't understand."

"He doesn't get to ride in like a white knight after four years, like nothing ever happened—"

"You happened. You." Hysteria tickled her throat; her legs quivered with the need to give out. "You threatened to take the house back again, didn't you? That's why he left."

Her father said nothing, confirming her fear and wrenching a pitiful sob from River's throat. Where had he gone? Oh God, what if he vanished again before she could reach him? No...it couldn't happen this way. Not after they'd gotten so close to having everything they'd ever dreamed of. Love. A family. No time limits.

"Didn't you ever stop to think how much Vaughn must love me, if he would leave behind everything familiar in a heartbeat, just so I would have a home? Or how much he must love me if joining the Army and getting sent overseas was the only way he could manage to stay away? Did you?" She had to get out of there. Had to go find him. "I want that kind of love for my daughter some day. I'm sorry you've let pride turn your heart black. Get out of my way."

River ran down the stairs, stopping in the kitchen long enough to assure herself Duke's sisters could watch Marcy until she returned. Then she kissed her daughter on both cheeks and went after her man.

Chapter Twenty-Two

River sat on the motel room bed, wondering if she'd gone insane. Three hours had passed since Vaughn drove away from the curb in front of her house. After confirming he hadn't returned to the motel, she'd checked the Third Shift, the factory construction site, Duke's house…but he'd been nowhere. Vanished. Again.

Somehow, she continued to have faith. Faith that he wouldn't leave her alone again after making so many vehement promises to the contrary. Most of all, there was a lit candle in her heart, refusing to go out. Maybe it had remained lit over his forty-nine month and three-day absence, too, nothing able to snuff it out. That certainty, that undying need to trust the man she loved, was what led River to renting a room at the motel. Not just any room, though. *Their* room. The room they'd met in so many times during their youth, making desperate love on the creaking mattress while traffic whooshed softly past in the background.

He would come. She *knew* he would. And she wouldn't let him have doubts or worries or reservations about staying in Hook, staying with her and Marcy. If it took forever, she would let him know their fate had been sealed in the Hook High parking lot, and she would never, ever, meet a better man as long as she lived. Just thinking of how helpless he must have felt with her home—a home he'd just needed more *time* and support to make for them—hanging in the balance…it made her entire body throb with pain.

Being in the same room with her worst memory wasn't easy. But she would pull out every stop to keep Vaughn from trying to be noble again. If they had to live in this very room to stay together, they would get through it. They would get better together. All three of them. Father, mother, and daughter. Because apart? They were loose ends that were meant to be tied.

When River heard a door slam out in the parking lot, she shot to her feet, her blood already flowing at warp speed. Squaring her shoulders, she went for the door and flung it open, halting Vaughn in his footsteps where he crossed the parking lot.

"Riv? What…" She watched as he registered the doorway she stood in, watched as he tried to decide why. Whatever conclusion he landed on, it propelled him toward the room, his big hand banding around River's elbow. "What are you doing in there, doll? I don't want you in there."

"I'm waiting for you." She pulled out of his hold and clasped the sides of his face. "Part of me has been here, waiting for you the whole time."

He fell onto River, giving her no choice but to walk them backward into the room, while Vaughn released heaving breaths into her neck. "I won't do it. I won't do it this time."

Every molecule in her body screamed to a halt. "Do what?"

"Leave. I refuse to leave again." His voice was rich and deep, just like the relief that clamored through River's blood, getting it running again. "I must be a selfish bastard, because I didn't even try." He lifted his head and searched her eyes. "Tell me why you're in this room. If you're trying to bring this full circle by ending things where I ended them, I've got news for you—it's not happening. Get it right out of your head. They'll have to take me away from this town—from my wife and child—in a coffin this time."

River's heart rejoiced, lifting and dancing inside her rib cage "Wife?"

"Yeah. *Wife*. Husband. Forever. No questions." She felt Vaughn's hand moving at their hips...and then he raised a ring between them. A gorgeous, old-fashioned, antique-looking ring that instantly became the most beautiful piece of jewelry she'd ever beheld, despite its slight tarnish. "I'm not going to lie, Riv. It's from a pawn shop. I'm a pawnshop guy, okay? But I won't be forever. I'm making good, doll. I'm going to make you proud of me. Proud to call me your man... and Marcy proud to call me dad."

Tears slipped down her cheeks, but the warmth felt good and healthy, so she didn't bother swiping them away. How could she focus on anything but the man in front of her? The startlingly gorgeous man she'd loved beyond reason since they'd first locked eyes. "I want to be your wife," she managed. "Of course I do. I'm in this room because I wanted to propose to you."

His mouth formed a lopsided smile. "What's that now?"

"I wanted to paint over the bad memory with something good. Something that should have always been." She held out her hand, laughing tearfully as he slipped the twisted silver onto her finger. "Vaughn, we can be a family anywhere. We don't need my parents' house. Or a house at all. We have love. That's more important than some pile of bricks. I *want* to do it on our own."

He pressed their foreheads together on a broken sound.

"You trust me that much, Riv?"

"Yes." She pushed up on her toes and kissed him, once, twice. "I didn't think you'd left town. Not for a single second. I knew I just had to wait and you'd come to me. I knew."

His breath released in a long rush. "Thank you. I don't know what I did to earn that kind of belief, but I'm going to fight like hell to keep it. I'm fighting already. No more secrets… just River and Vaughn. All in." No sooner were the words out of his mouth than he started backing River toward the bed, groaning when she fell across the mattress, and teasing the hem of her dress with coarse fingertips. "Tell me you love me."

Lightness invaded her chest. "I love you."

"Tell me you know we can do this."

"I know we can do this. We can do anything."

Vaughn closed his eyes a moment, as if savoring the words where they hung in the air. Then he fell forward, planting his fists on either side of River's thighs, bending down to snap his teeth at her belly button. "Now, tell me to fuck you."

River's nipples went so stiff, such wetness rushing to the juncture of her thighs, she released a loud whimper. "Fuck me, please."

Using one fist to keep himself propped above her, Vaughn reached down and undid his belt and fly, loosing his erection from his pants, where it hung between them like a promise. River parted her thighs, running greedy hands over her breasts while repeating the words he'd asked her to say. Chanting them.

Finally, Vaughn sunk down between her legs, rocking into the valley between them, stretching River's arms above her head and anchoring them there. "Took your innocence in this bed. Got you pregnant in this bed." His mouth skated down the side of her neck. "Took you rough both times, didn't I? So rough."

"You always do," River panted, sliding her feet up and

down his backside.

"I always will, doll." His mouth worked the buttons of her dress, popping them free as he thrust against the cradle of her body, guarded only by her panties. "But the first time I take you wearing my ring, it's going to be slow. If you can't feel how much I fucking love you in every drive of my cock, you tell me, so I can slow down even more. You with me?"

"*Yes.*"

Vaughn transferred his grip on her wrists to his right hand, using the left to remove her panties with painstaking care, testing her wetness the same way, until River was a writhing, begging mess on the bed. She strained in her fiancé's hold as he covered his column of flesh with latex. Eager. So eager.

"Oh, please…" His first pump into her body was far from gentle. No, he filled her with a vengeance, in one swift drive, grunting loudly into her neck. After that, though…it was all slow, grinding movements, rolling River's eyes to the back of her head.

"My wife. My River." His mouth worked hers over with desperate glides of his tongue. His eyes were pinched so tightly shut that River felt moisture gather behind her own. And all the while he entered her with powerful but unhurried thrusts. "You feel my love?"

"I feel it," she gasped.

"You'll never be without it another day." His breath bathed her lips. "You never have been. I've loved you up one side of forever. Now I'm going to love you back down the other."

"I'll love you forever, too."

"*River.*" The rolls of his hips grew jerky, frantic. "*Don't let go of me.*"

"*Never.* Never again.*"

Epilogue

Someone once said it takes a village to raise a child. Or maybe just a house full of divorcées…and their extremely patient brother, who honestly just wanted to watch SportsCenter.

River's father hadn't thrown them out of the house after all, but River, Vaughn, and Marcy had moved out one week ago, despite the older man's concession. Without Vaughn having to say a word, River had understood his reluctance to depend on her father's act of kindness—and while River and Vaughn had accepted an apology from the man who'd raised her, she shared Vaughn's urgency to be an independent unit.

They had a while to go before they could afford a house of their own, however, so they were paying weekly rent to Duke and living in the two-bedroom guest house across his backyard. Just for now.

At first they'd been hesitant about imposing, but they'd been given no choice, coming downstairs one morning to find Duke and his sisters packing up the living room of River's house. It had taken some shuffling of the sisters—two of them were now sharing a bedroom—but Marcy had already thrived in the boisterous, family-oriented environment. Even Duke had volunteered for babysitting duty, which had led to a quiet bond between Marcy and the giant mechanic. Just the other night, River and Vaughn had come home from a rare date night to find Marcy passed out beside Duke on the couch, a football highlight reel playing on the television.

Today was Vaughn's first official day working at the factory. He stood in front of the bathroom mirror, Marcy sitting on the vanity with her teddy bear, River fixing the deep blue tie she'd bought him. He would be addressing the factory floor today and going over the new safety procedures he and his partner Milo had put into place. Oddly enough, Vaughn wasn't the least bit nervous. What did he have to be apprehensive about when he had the unwavering support of a family he'd never dared envision? God, they were…his everything. And when he looked into River's eyes, he knew she wasn't going anywhere. Four years apart might have been utter hell, but they were strong in the wake of his absence. They weren't losing each other again.

River still worked her assembly line job, but after confiding in Vaughn she missed challenging her mind, she'd enrolled in night classes twice a week. Her goal was to earn her bachelor's degree—no matter how long it took—and an eventual promotion to floor manager at the factory. And while Vaughn still held on to the staunch belief River had the potential for more, he *felt* her happiness, right in the center of his chest. When River said she wouldn't be happy anywhere but with him and Marcy, he believed her, the way he should have done years earlier. They weren't living in the past now, though. Only the present, while looking forward to the bright future they planned to give their daughter.

"We got pancakes on over here!" One of Duke's sisters yelled from down in the backyard. "Chocolate chips. You know anyone who likes those?"

Marcy's entire body began to wiggle on the sink. "Daddy, can I go?"

A beat passed while Vaughn figured out how to speak around the golf ball lodged in his throat. "Yeah, kiddo." He lifted his daughter off the sink, following her to the door to make sure she got across the yard all right. Before she went down the steps, Marcy turned and hugged his right leg, then took off running.

River's arms banded around his middle right on time, keeping him from bursting wide open with all of the contentment and pride and love. So many emotions he'd never expected to feel after leaving Hook. Leaving River.

He picked up River's left hand and examined the simple gold wedding band he'd slid onto her finger at a civil ceremony in city hall. Neither one of them had been interested in waiting—not after they'd waited four long years to be together—so they'd recited their vows on a rainy afternoon while Marcy colored in the front row of the judge's chamber, Duke serving as their witness. When Vaughn thought back to the ceremony, which had taken place mere days after they'd reunited in the motel, all he could remember was the blue of River's eyes, how tears had swam in them, and gravity tugged him closer until they were forehead to forehead, sharing the same oxygen. Exactly where he wanted to remain for the rest of his life.

"We're going to buy ourselves a house, Riv. For Marcy. For us." He turned in her hold, sliding their mouths together. "It won't be long."

"I don't care how long it takes, or how many hours we have to work." The ends of her blonde hair tickled his shoulders. "We already have everything worth working for. The rest is extra."

Needing more contact—always, always—Vaughn stooped down, wedging a forearm beneath River's ass and lifting her against his body. He tilted his hips forward a little to remind her they would be meeting in the machine room on their mutual lunch break, and she nodded in unspoken agreement.

"We're going to get caught someday." Her laugh was shaky, even as her legs wrapped around his waist. "We can't keep—"

"Can't?" Vaughn lifted an eyebrow and emitted a low growl. "Don't you know better by now than to tell me I can't do something, doll?"

"Maybe I do." River's tongue slid across the fullness of her bottom lip, challenge lighting in the eyes he saw in his dreams, even with her sleeping right beside him. "Maybe telling my husband he can't do something is how I guarantee the opposite."

He took a few steps and propped River up against the wall, swallowing the moan she let loose. "Crafty woman."

She tore away from the kiss, a teasing smile curling the edges of her mouth. "You *can't* blow me a kiss at the end of your speech this morning. You can't let me pack you a lunch with a cute note on the napkin…and show all your friends—"

Their warm chuckles were lost in the ensuing tongue kiss, but kicked back up when Vaughn tickled River's ribs with his fingertips. "You're abusing your power. It should be used for good, not evil."

"Yeah?" River whispered, her sweet smile turning dreamy. "You *can't* love me forever. You *can't* sleep beside me every night for the rest of my life."

Vaughn heaved a breath into his wife's soft neck. "Aw, doll. Just try and stop me."

Acknowledgments

Thank you to so many people.

Patrick and Mackenzie, loves of my life. Like River, Vaughn and Marcy, we are also a really special work in progress and I treasure every minute we spend yelling, laughing and collapsed from exhaustion.

Heather Howland, my editor at Entangled. We've done so many books together and this rhythm of editing stories has become such a comforting process. We've come a long way from swapping POVs, removing the weird NA storylines and making my heroes sound less like stalkers (read: Protecting What's His).

Christine, my aunt. For being the most badass single mother I know, putting yourself through night school while raising a child and holding down a full time job—you inspired this story.

Stephanie Lapensee, my publicist at Inkslinger. I appreciate your time and energy so much. What an unexpected bonus that you like the books!

Sara Eirew, photographer extraordinare. This cover is

divine, because of your talent.

Eagle, beta reader, endangered bird. You say nice things. I like them.

Bailey's Babes, my FB reader's group. I love our fun, not-so-little club and its positivity. For a friendship founded on bulge pics, we are pretty damn mighty.

About the Author

New York Times and USA TODAY bestselling author Tessa Bailey lives in Brooklyn, New York, with her husband and young daughter. When she isn't writing or reading romance, she enjoys a good argument and thirty-minute recipes.

www.tessabailey.com
Join Bailey's Babes!

RAW REDEMPTION

BOILING POINT

OWNED BY FATE

EXPOSED BY FATE

DRIVEN BY FATE

TELL ME YOU CRAVE ME
a *Search and Seduce* novel by Joya Ryan

Easton Ambrose has always protected Natalie St. Clair from guys like himself, but what's he supposed to do when she insists on going out with the wrong kind of guy? Kiss her, of course. Worst idea in the history of bad ideas. She's his best friend's little sister. But now Natalie won't take no for an answer—even if it's bound to blow up in their faces. Because even if they survive their bedroom antics, it's only a matter of time before they're caught…

LOVERS RESTORED
a novel by Kelsie Leverich

Halle Morgan returned to her hometown for the first time in ten years, only to find there is no escape from the past…or from the man she wants like no other. Cooper Bale has been drowning in painful memories. Still, he can't forget Halle and the bittersweet night they once shared. Even now, insatiable longing sizzles between them. Though blissful nights spent in Halle's arms heal the bitterness in Cooper's heart, they know they have no future. Not until they let go of the past that brought them together.

Printed in Great Britain
by Amazon